Y0-AJV-358

```
J          Terris, Susan.
FIC           Author! Author! / Susan Terris. -- New York :
Terri      Farrar, Straus, Giroux, 1990.
              167 p.

           04278941   LC:89046389   ISBN:0374349959

           I. Title


975      91JUN10                  20/ax    1-00968190
```

*Author! Author!*

*Also by Susan Terris*

NELL'S QUILT
THE LATCHKEY KIDS
BABY-SNATCHER
OCTOPUS PIE
WINGS AND ROOTS
NO SCARLET RIBBONS
STAGE BRAT
TUCKER AND THE HORSE THIEF
THE CHICKEN POX PAPERS
TWO P'S IN A POD
THE PENCIL FAMILIES
PICKLE
WHIRLING RAINBOWS
PLAGUE OF FROGS
THE DROWNING BOY
ON FIRE

# Author! Author!

— SUSAN TERRIS —

FARRAR · STRAUS · GIROUX
NEW YORK

Copyright © 1990 by Susan Terris
All rights reserved
Library of Congress catalog card number: 89-46389
Published simultaneously in Canada
by HarperCollins*CanadaLtd*
Printed in the United States of America
Designed by Martha Rago
First edition, 1990

*You Are My Sunshine*
by Jimmie Davis and Charles Mitchell
Copyright © 1940 Peer International Corporation
Copyright renewed
International copyright secured
All rights reserved
Used by permission

*TO MYRA*
*who was wise enough to refuse to take part
in any of my searches for early success*

*Author! Author!*

# 1

*It was a shimmering hot day. Annalisa wanted to swing by her knees from a tree or swim in the ocean. But, when the pelican with the broken wing croaked, she dropped the magic butter churn and forgot to be hot. Her adventure was beginning . . .*

"Oh, no," Valerie gasped, flipping through the rest of the pages. "Did I write that?"

With a sigh, she turned to the yellow endpaper, scribbled her name, and closed the book. Yes, she—Valerie Meyerson—*had* written this story about a girl called Annalisa and a magic butter churn. Then, thanks to a poet named Tekla Reis, the New York firm of Sverdrup & Liebson had published it. That was the good part. The embarrassing part was that she'd written it five years ago when she was only seven. Her first novel had become a thirty-two-page children's picture book. Now every word she'd labored over in Miss Burdette's second-grade composition class was being examined and picked apart from coast to coast.

"Val, are you with us?" a voice asked.

She blinked and rubbed her eyes. It was her father's edgy voice breaking into her consciousness. He and her mother were uncomfortable with her newfound literary celebrity, referring to her as "our changeling" and insisting that they weren't sure where she'd come from. Valerie was suspicious of this reference. Her parents were middle-management bankers who seldom mentioned anything as poetic as a changeling, usually preferring to confine themselves to discussions about skill sets, number-crunching, and quarterly reports. The last book they'd both read, besides hers, was *West with the Night*; and they tackled it because they were having dinner with someone who was supposed to be Beryl Markham's stepgrandson.

Today, looking somewhat out of place, they'd brought Valerie to Open Sesame for her first book-signing party. As Alix, the energetic bookstore owner with dimpled elbows, strode around in bunny slippers dealing out carrot sticks and cups of cider, her red-haired six-foot-seven assistant, Hatch, waved a stubby pencil and tried to keep the crowd in order. Well, it wasn't a crowd exactly. Along with Valerie's parents, other autograph party attendees included Tekla Reis, Val's aunt DeDe, her cousin Bennett, some of her seventh-grade classmates, and a reporter from the *San Francisco Chronicle*. Valerie's editor, Molly Moore, who was in town for a conference, was there, but—after patting Val on the head once or twice as if she were a terrier not yet finished with obedience school—Molly had seemed more interested in discussing other people's books with Tekla and Alix.

Someone in a blazer that looked as if it were coated

with split-pea soup and bits of ham touched her arm. It was the *Chronicle* reporter. "Val," he said, "we'd like to shoot you with your parents and Ms. Reis."

Obligingly Valerie slid down from the stool and stepped forward. Although she would have liked to suggest that she be photographed only with Tekla Reis, she didn't.

"Here. Over here," a voice commanded.

A man with two cameras around his neck was pushing her back against a display of copies of *The Magic Butter Churn*. Her mother and father, upholstered in well-cut flannel, were being wedged in next to her. Valerie took a deep breath, but she felt as if she weren't getting enough air. She could see Tekla Reis moving slowly in their direction, almost as if she were swimming toward them instead of using her feet. Tekla seemed unruffled by the situation.

"This is all wrong," the reporter moaned, picking a shred of ham off one split-pea lapel. "It's not going to read right."

Valerie looked down. She had, for once, forgotten how tall she was. Of course it wasn't going to read right. At twelve, Val's dark-haired, scarecrow self towered over Stan and Claire Meyerson, those short, rounded blond people who were her parents.

"Bring the stool over. Sit her on that."

Valerie did as she was told, but the stool made it worse. Now she loomed even higher over her parents' heads. Tekla hadn't yet joined the tableau. She stood to one side with her head cocked and a thin-lipped, unreadable expression on her face.

"Get a chair," Molly Moore suggested, abandoning her discussion with Alix and moving forward.

5

"Dig a hole," squawked someone. Her cousin Bennett, perhaps. Or one of her classmates.

Valerie blinked nervously. People were laughing, and she was beginning to perspire. Alix put down the carrot sticks and screeched a chair toward them across the vinyl floor. Valerie wanted to screech, too. Her autograph party had hardly begun, and it looked as if it was going to be a disaster. She wanted to go home, but her parents were behind her, each with a hand on her shoulder. Valerie wasn't sure whether this was a gesture of affection or one intended to ensure that she didn't try to flee.

Tekla, twisting the strand of dark yellow beads that hung around her neck, was still idling off to one side.

"Ms. Reis," the reporter wheedled, with a sweeping gesture, "we do need you to join the family."

Tekla nodded and, releasing her beads, she joined them. Claire's fingers dug into Valerie's shoulder. Val tried to angle her head so she could see the expression on her mother's face, but her father, who was humming, lifted his hand and swiveled her head foward again.

"Closer, Ms. Reis. Move in. Mr. Meyerson, put your left shoulder back so we can get a tight shot with Ms. Reis and your family."

Valerie couldn't see her mother, her father, or Tekla Reis anymore, and this made her feel anxious. Valerie had met Tekla only nine months ago at Rossi Pool, but her parents and Tekla had been good friends for years before Val was born. These days the three of them were cordial to one another, but they no longer did things together, and sometimes a shadow of disapproval flickered across her parents' faces when Tekla's name was mentioned.

"Still tighter, Ms. Reis. Close that gap."

Valerie tried to forget the group behind her and concentrate on what was occurring before her eyes. While she was being photographed, she made mental snapshots of everyone. Molly Moore had a carrot stick propped between her fingers as if it were a cigarette. Her eyes behind their oversized glasses were darting from side to side as if she—like Val—were plotting escape routes from Open Sesame. Molly seemed to regret that she'd flown west without a mask and a tank of New York smog to breathe. Click.

Not far from Molly Moore was Valerie's cousin Bennett, a college freshman who was given to curling his lip and uttering barbs appropriate—or inappropriate—to every occasion. Bennett always had some girl in tow. He seemed to select them by name. They were mostly Kates, with an occasional Wendy included for variety. The new Kate was dressed in black and had a bowler hat on her head. Click.

Valerie's classmates were peering curiously at her as if she were the largest primate in the zoo, as if the afternoon at Open Sesame were just another field trip, which it was, since her English teacher, Mr. Litke, had posted a sign-up sheet in the front hall. While Val was examining them, she realized that Jo Samuels, her sometimes best friend, wasn't there. The others had probably come to get out of history and P.E. She fixed her attention on their faces. Click. If she'd had a Magic Marker, she might have scribbled mustaches on them.

Squinting, she raised a hand and rubbed at her nose. Click.

"Put your hand down, Valerie. Just one more," the photographer barked. Click. "Yes. Fine. That's it. Thanks."

Tekla moved off and began to flip through some paperback books. Val's parents edged away in the opposite direction.

"Questions?" Alix asked. "More apple juice? How about answering some questions, Val? And you won't mind if I videotape this, will you?"

Valerie swallowed. Questions? A videotape? Why hadn't someone warned her? Aware of a rising sense of desperation, she scanned the room, hoping Molly Moore would help her with the questions, but Molly was out on the sidewalk smoking either the carrot stick or a small orangish cigar.

"Questions?" Alix repeated brightly. "Hey, you're not that bashful. Now, who wants to begin? Ask how she gets her ideas. Who she models her characters on."

"How do you get your ideas? Who do you model your characters on?" The boy who'd mouthed the questions was someone named Barry or Larry.

"Author! Author!" Bennett called out, stomping one foot. "Let's hear from the author."

Valerie squinted. Bennett was making fun of her. Had Larry/Barry been mocking her, too? Her hands were dangling heavily at the ends of her arms, and she didn't know where to put them. "My ideas, my characters," she mumbled, aware of an uncontrollable wobble in her voice.

"Yes," Alix prodded. "Or tell us where you do your best thinking."

"What?"

Alix smiled. "Say the first thing that comes to mind."

"In the bathtub," Val replied, without pausing to take a breath.

Giggles and snorts rippled through the crowd. Valerie reeled up her hands and slid them halfway into her pockets. Had she really said "bathtub," encouraging her classmates to picture her body naked and submerged in water? And why? Because she was nervous. Because this was the first time she'd appeared publicly as an *author*.

"I didn't mean that," she said, attempting to repair the damage she'd done. "I do my best thinking at my desk. The rolltop. With a yellow tablet and a number 3 pencil. Not in the bathtub. Never in the bathtub. I never take a bath."

Val's classmates, startled by her awkwardness, exploded with laughter. Then they began to jabber and press closer. She felt like a caged animal.

"Did you really write *The Magic Butter Churn* when you were *seven?*"

"Why is the prince bald? I thought princes were supposed to be handsome."

"A river of butter? A ride in a pelican's mouth?"

"Well . . ." Valerie said, struggling to compose herself. "I wanted to be original. I was trying to say something important." She swallowed hard. She was lying. She'd written the story so long ago, she didn't remember what she'd intended. Why was she here? What was she doing?

At that moment, Tekla Reis, brooding, took a step forward. Her frowning face was framed by a halo of dark hair. Val turned toward her parents and found them inching closer to her, too.

"Being an author is hard," Valerie said, leaning away

from her parents and speaking directly to Tekla. "Writing isn't easy."

Tekla nodded, but Val's classmates were muttering, and their questions were becoming challenges.

"Why does Annalisa turn into a pelican?"

"How come she has to build a nest and eat fish?"

"Did you really write that when you were seven?"

"Maybe she wrote it last month."

"Maybe her mother wrote it."

Valerie rolled her head from side to side. Her mouth was so full of saliva, she was afraid she was going to start drooling. She couldn't seem to swallow or speak. Nor could she get enough air. She felt as if someone were holding her head under water, waiting for her to turn blue.

Then she heard Jo Samuels's voice. "Val did write that book. I remember. I was in Miss Burdette's class with her."

So Jo had come. Once, before Val had been consumed by the excitement of having a book published, she could have scanned any crowd and located her. Now Jo seemed more like a casual acquaintance and was, Val realized, beginning to sound that way, also. "But . . . the story's different," Jo continued. "The pelican's funnier, and I'm not sure the river was butter. I remember a prince, but he wasn't a bald prince. He was a *bad* prince, and he—"

"Stop!" Valerie begged, stiffening as she eyed the increasingly hostile audience. She couldn't locate Tekla Reis. Maybe, disgusted, she'd left. And where were Val's parents, Alix, and Molly Moore? Why was she facing this ordeal alone?

Suddenly unable to hold herself in check, she jumped

there were an invisible sheet of Plexiglas separating her from the three of them.

Valerie glanced at the review. It said that the illustrations by the famous New York artist were "luminous" and Val's prose was "naïvely amusing." It also said that, "although young, she appeared to have already honed to perfection her own brilliant version of artistic volatility." Cringing, Valerie realized that the *Chronicle* reporter had seen her fall apart. She hadn't even had the good sense to faint or pretend to be ill. Instead, Hatch and her father had dragged her off shouting. It was on videotape, too. Every word she'd uttered.

Her parents would forgive her. They always did. They'd endured so many childless years, as her mother suffered one miscarriage after another before she'd appeared in their lives, that they'd never stopped treating her like a rare flower that had bloomed on their doorstep. Still, there was something inattentive and off-base about their attitudes. Now, for instance, they were taking her talent for granted and focusing only on their conviction that the book publication was putting too much pressure on her. Well, maybe they were right. It had caused her to behave so badly that the idea of having to face her classmates at Horton Middle School again made her feel sick.

But things were going to be different. It would be a long time before Valerie wore a Laura Ashley dress again or appeared at another book signing for *The Magic Butter Churn*. In fact, she'd put that book out of her head and start to write a real novel. Maybe she'd give up on trying to be young or cute, since it didn't work anyway, and focus on looking more like Bennett's newest Kate. Dressed in black with a hat tamping down her hair, she'd look literary and sophisticated.

Her parents wouldn't understand, but Tekla Reis probably would, just as Tekla would agree that Valerie needed a serious subject to write about. Perhaps she should write about her lost twin. Often Val felt as if she and some shadowy twin sister had been separated at birth. Or that there was another mystery to her life. Something she needed to unravel.

Valerie stared at the soggy, wrinkled brown flakes clinging to the bottom and sides of her cereal bowl. She narrowed her eyes, trying to decode their meaning as if they were tea leaves in which she could read the past or the future. Honest people seldom said she looked like either Claire or Stan Meyerson. And her parents did make that joke about her being their changeling. Perhaps she'd been accidentally switched in the hospital nursery. Maybe—in addition to being a twin—she was a changeling, like the ugly duckling. That would explain why her parents were so fair and she was so dark. Why they were so calm and ordinary and she was so intense.

# 2

*Saralinda could hardly contain herself. Finally, she was about to be reunited with her long-lost twin, Margolite. Although the twins had come into the world as royal offspring, they'd been wrenched apart at birth, separated by fate and circumstance, when all they wanted was . . .*

"Chlorine," Tekla Reis muttered, inhaling air from the hand cupped over her nose and mouth. "No matter what I do or how I wash, I reek of it. My soul, too, is chlorinated, slowly bleaching out yet unable to rid itself of a telltale, poisonous green tinge."

Valerie sniffled and clung to the gutter at the deep end of the swimming pool. She'd been swimming laps for twenty minutes already, thinking about her new novel and wondering if Tekla would appear. Now she'd shown up, yet before she'd even put her feet in the water, she was off on a tirade that Val only dimly understood.

Without turning her head, Valerie tried to examine Tekla. All she saw, however, was a distorted glimpse of a lowered head, a navy Speedo, and legs that were feathered with dark hair. Tekla, she'd learned, didn't like to be looked at directly. Val wasn't sure, but thought it might be something like the way it was with gorillas. If you gazed into their eyes, they felt they were being challenged. Peripheral glances, on the other hand, were expected and tolerated as a proper gesture of submission. And Tekla, after all, was a well-known poet, even if she hadn't published a book in almost ten years.

Tekla slid forward so the soles of her feet were slapping against the surface of the water. She sniffed at her fingers again. "Lady Macbeth would've understood my need to rid myself of this permeating stench."

"I think it's nice," Val said, "like the smell of clean clothes. Besides, why do you swim if you hate it so much?"

Tekla blinked and flicked a spray like cold porcupine quills in Valerie's direction. Stung by the puzzling gesture, Val submerged and resumed her laps of breaststroke. Pull, kick, glide. Pull, kick, glide.

This particular day, Val decided, was an inconvenient one for Tekla to turn moody or biting. Since she had alienated Jo Samuels and every friend she'd ever had on Friday when she'd made that scene at Open Sesame, she'd begun to hope that her relationship with Tekla could assume a new importance and that the poet would be able to help her with the mysteries that seemed to surround her life. Sunday was a good day to begin, too, because none of Val's Horton swim team members were there. Coming to practice on their one free day wasn't considered cool. Well, Val wasn't interested in being cool. She wanted someone to talk to.

Tekla was in the pool now, stroking behind her in

the lane marked MEDIUM. Valerie reached the end, did a somersault turn, and glided forward underwater. Opening her eyes, she peered upward at Tekla approaching on her left. The body like hers, long and thin, in its tank suit, the dark hair drifting upward in the aquamarine fluid. Tekla's eyes were closed but her mouth was open as if she were screaming. Instead of noise, however, a long stream of bubbles escaped from between her teeth.

As the two of them passed, their wakes merged, bobbing their bodies into a moment of contact. Valerie slowed down, trying to picture Tekla at her age or as she was when her parents first knew her. When Val reached the end of the pool, she squatted in the shallow water, staring at Tekla and wondering what it would be like to have her as a mother.

Tekla was not beautiful, but she had a high-cheeked, exotic glamour that Val found appealing. According to Val's father, Tekla came from a very literary family. Her grandfather had been a famous novelist, her mother a prominent editor, and her brother was a playwright. Tekla's first collection of poems had been published when she was nineteen and had already graduated from Radcliffe.

As Val watched Tekla, she found herself thinking of the breakers at Ocean Beach and the heady sound of cymbals being clapped together. "Tekla Reis," she whispered. "Tekla Jane Reis." Surely that was a more distinctive name and less singsongy than Valerie Meyerson.

"Speaking to me?" Tekla asked as she glided up.

"No, not really," Val mumbled, turning sideways in confusion.

Tekla raised her head and shook excess water from her hair. "I'm sorry I was bitchy, but I'm feeling rotten today. And, in any case, my reaction to chlorine is always the worst before I get in. When I'm swimming, I love it. It's like returning to the womb—all that whooshing in warm liquid . . ."

Val nodded, but thought she should avoid committing herself to an answer.

Tekla, who seemed to agree, lifted a pair of blue foam kickboards from the tile at the edge of the pool and floated one over to Valerie.

"I started this when I read your stuff and showed it to Molly. But I'm not used to spending time around twelve-year-olds, and I think I've made a mistake. Early success is a mixed blessing—I know, because I've been there. It tends to make a person into a monumental pain in the ass."

Valerie wrapped her arms around the board. "I'm trying not to be that way, but I am starting a novel about my life. It seems to be full of mysteries. Sometimes I think I'm a changeling or adopted. I mean, for instance, why don't I look like my parents? I look more like you than I do like either of them. Have you noticed? Probably not, but—still—I'm afraid I can't get what's in my head out on paper. I'm not sure I'll be able to do anything really good."

"You wrote *The Magic Butter Churn.*"

Val nodded. "But that was five years ago, and I was a different person then."

The corners of Tekla's mouth curved upward, but her eyes were wary. "You're an interesting child. Well, go on—do it. Write your novel. But make sure you show it to me."

"Yes," Val said. "I will. Because I want, if I can, to be just like you."

Tekla groaned. Then she pushed off, gliding as far as possible before beginning to practice flutter kicks. Valerie, imitating her, did the same thing. When she and Tekla reached the far end of the pool, Tekla took a deep breath and continued speaking. "Val, don't try to be like me. Be like you. What do *you* think? What's important to you? Observe and be ruthless. Stretch. Put your soul into your work."

Valerie turned toward Tekla and grinned at her. "Even if it's tinged with chlorine?"

"What?"

"Your soul. I was making a joke. Isn't that what you said before—that your soul had turned green from the chlorine?"

"Oh, God, what am I doing and how am I going to deal with all this? Children are so literal. Do you carry a waterproof pen and notebook tucked up one flank of your bathing suit?"

"Don't get mad, Tekla, please. I want us to be friends. Good friends. Sometimes—I know it's ridiculous—but sometimes I even wish you were my mother."

Tekla stared at Valerie for a moment. Then, flinging the kickboard out of the pool, she submerged, resurfaced in the FAST lane, and began to churn her way through the water with a fierce, choppy freestyle stroke. Val backed up, hooked one elbow over the second rung of the ladder, and watched her. Tekla was taking six, sometimes seven, strokes before she rolled her head for air. Instinctively, Valerie found she was holding her breath every time Tekla held hers. Val was the breath-holding champion of the Horton team. She'd been clocked at 2:25, but she was running out of air long before Tekla.

Tekla, who usually swam only in an elegant, leisurely manner, was attacking the water with open palms, struggling in a way that was hindering her forward progress. Valerie wanted to lunge at Tekla when she thrashed by, grab her arm, and apologize, but she was afraid. Forcing herself to look away, she moved hand over hand up to the bronze ladder and hauled herself up out of the pool. She was going to head for the showers.

As she stripped off her goggles and used two fingers to pull down the bottom of her suit, she turned back toward the pool. In the far corner, the lifeguard seemed to be doing homework. Two men in the MEDIUM lane had stopped to talk. A fleshy older woman in SLOW was on her back staring at the ceiling as she sculled along with her hands. And Tekla Reis was—no, Tekla Reis wasn't blasting her way down the FAST lane.

Valerie leaned forward and peered down. Under the water in the deepest part of the pool she saw some kind of dense, round blur.

"Oh, no," she gasped.

Then, springing forward, she dove, pulling herself down and forward as fast as she could. It was Tekla under there, Tekla curved into a jellyfish position somewhere just above the drain.

But as Val submerged, Tekla began to float upward. When they collided, Val grabbed hold of Tekla's waist. She kicked, flailing with her free arm, until they both broke the surface of the water.

Tekla was gasping and coughing. "Stop. Let go."

Reluctantly Valerie released her. Tekla dog-paddled toward the ladder as Val sculled behind her.

"I was coming up," Tekla said, grabbing for the gutter. "The heroics weren't necessary. I was just . . . just momentarily dizzy." Between each syllable, Tekla was breathing in and out hoarsely.

"Everything okay?" the lifeguard inquired, looking up from his notebook.

"Yes," Val growled. Then she closed the gap between herself and Tekla. "Do you need help getting out?" she asked.

"No," Tekla said. Then she twisted back and nodded. "Well, maybe. Yes. Okay. Why not. You want to be grownup, be grownup. Go on, help me . . ."

As the hot water needled down on their heads, Valerie stretched the straps to help Tekla peel the Speedo from her body. She squeezed the excess water out of the suit and hung it upside down on a hook.

Two people in a shower stall felt awkward. "I should go now," Val said.

Tekla propped herself against the gray tile wall. "No, wait. I'm still dizzy. Step out, but stay close."

Valerie did as she'd been told. She swaddled herself in her towel and stood outside the stall, remembering to observe Tekla only from an angle. Even from an angle, she was aware that Tekla's body, although slim, had flesh that was dimpled, rippled, and ribbed with stretch marks like Claire's body. It had a scar, too, a long one that marked her torso from the rib cage to the groin.

Tekla turned, facing the rear wall, and leaned forward to let the hot water cascade down her back. "If I admit to the idea that you might have rescued me, then I am in your power forever."

"You were coming up," Val told her.

"That's what I'll choose to believe, too," Tekla said, speaking over one shoulder. "And I'll tell you something else as well. Tell you everything, since you seem to be in such a hurry to grow up. I'm not myself today. I'm taking very badly to the notion of my approaching menopause. As if my body's becoming an enemy camp. Now I bleed and bleed for nothing, until I feel like hell, am anemic, then get spaced out when I try to swim a few energetic laps."

Valerie wondered if she should bite her tongue and keep quiet, but she felt reckless. "Those weren't energetic laps," she declared. "You were punishing yourself for something. Or me. What's wrong, Tekla? Don't you want to be friends?"

Tekla leaned back against the tile again. She whistled. "You are surprising. You are—hey, what are you looking at?"

"Huh? Oh. Nothing." She'd been examining Tekla's abdominal scar.

Tekla reached for her oversize towel and draped it around herself like a cloak. "I had a very big appendix," she said, with a dismissive wave. "But, Val, listen—I think you should know, my friends don't call me Tekla. They all call me T.J. Or—occasionally—just T."

# 3

*Meanwhile, Princess Tatiana—the twins' mother—distraught that potato-faced peasant children had been left at the castle in place of her daughters, fled from the king and sought refuge in a monastery run by Trappist monks. There, mourning her lost babies, she meditated in silence and wrote anguished poems about . . .*

". . . a Borsalino hat?" Stan Meyerson asked. "Claire, was that *my* Borsalino I saw on her head this morning?"

Self-consciously, Valerie fingered the brim of the black hat she'd found on the top shelf of the storage closet. "Yes," she whispered.

"Val?"

"What?" She edged from the hall where she'd been lingering into the kitchen.

Claire put down her coffee mug. "I hate it when you eavesdrop. But wait a minute. Isn't that my black turtleneck? The one that was in the sewing pile? First it's your dad's hat, and now it's my sweater. What's going on here? It's not Halloween already, is it?"

Valerie, staring at a refrigerator magnet that held the

newspaper clipping of her with Tekla and her parents, shrugged.

As she was trying to decide how to answer, her father reached out, angling the hat so it dipped down over her left eye. "It's quite nice, actually. Your gramp, who gave me that hat when I graduated from college, would be happy to know it's being put to good use. On you it looks very . . . literary. Oh, I see, this must be the day you're reading your book in assembly."

Valerie gulped. In her effort to prepare herself to face Horton Middle School again, she'd forgotten the assembly. Whether dressed in Laura Ashley flowers or in black, she could not imagine standing before her schoolmates to read *The Magic Butter Churn* out loud. What had she been thinking of when she'd told Mr. Singleton she'd do it?

"Come on, Ducky. Get your cereal, and—if you want a lift—shake a leg," her father urged. "I have a presentation to make this morning, and I can't be late."

"I'm not hungry."

Her parents wouldn't be at school to hear her, because it hadn't occurred to them to take time off from the bank for a middle-school program. When Claire, at age twelve, had been figure-skating, had her parents ever missed any performance she'd been in? If Tekla were Val's mother, she wouldn't have acted so insensitively. Tekla, however, didn't know of this event, because Val hadn't mentioned it. But in the future, things would be different, because she'd consult with her before she made terrible mistakes, like agreeing to read a seven-year-old's story before middle-school students.

"Maybe I should stay home," Val said, trying to decide why looking at the clipping bothered her. "School is the pits. I'm thinking of quitting the swim team, too."

Her mother frowned. "Your friends will be understanding. We were. But come on, grab your stuff. We've got to go."

Valerie slumped in the back of the Saab, clutching her books and yellow legal pad to her chest. Raising one hand, she tugged at the brim of the black felt hat. She'd have to find a way to escape the Horton assembly. But she couldn't discuss that with her parents, who, at moments like these, she often thought of as Stan and Claire, instead of as Mom and Dad.

In the front seat, Stan and Claire were murmuring among themselves. She was asking him about his stomach.

"Another flare-up?"

"Not too bad, but Mort wants to increase the Prednisone again. It's the pressure of this damned report. The projections seem contaminated. We may have a virus in the program."

Stan Meyerson had colitis, some kind of banker's ailment, nothing a person wanted to discuss in public. Claire's banker's condition was pain and swelling in her feet. Valerie considered these recurring symptoms unromantic and uninteresting. When Tekla had spoken to Val about *her* discomfort, she'd referred to menopause as a betrayal, something that had turned her body into an enemy camp. Somehow that seemed much more significant than diarrhea or sore feet.

"Val, answer. Do we have a bad connection? Or are you on temporary hold?"

"I'm here," Val said.

"We were asking you again about Swim Camp. You are planning to sign up, aren't you?"

For next summer? It was January, and they wanted to discuss June. By then Valerie would probably be working on her next novel. "No."

Claire glanced over one shoulder. "No?"

"No."

Stan reached back and patted her knee. "Well, we can take that up sometime when you're feeling more talkative. It alarms me when you're quiet, instead of your usual magpie self. Don't be nervous about the assembly. You'll do fine."

"You'll be wonderful," Claire chimed in.

Valerie made a face. She wouldn't be wonderful, and she thought perhaps she'd never chatter like a magpie again. Tekla didn't speak a lot, except when she had something important to say. Val thought that she might want to learn to cultivate silence, too. Starting with this morning.

When Val turned her head, she realized that Claire had already stopped the Saab in front of her school. "Wow them," she urged. "And remember, we love you. Oh, and listen, when you take off my sweater this afternoon, put it back in the sewing pile. It has a little rip under one arm."

Valerie reached out and pulled the handle of the back door. She gave the door a shove, but it swung back against her knees as she was poking her fingertips into her armpits searching for the rip.

It was under the left arm, but it wasn't little. Well, it was too late to do anything except keep her elbow clamped against her side. She slid out of the car and kicked the door closed with one foot.

Standing on the sidewalk with other students shouting and shoving around her, Valerie was trying to determine how long she had to wait before she turned and ran home. The decision was taken out of her hands as Mr. Singleton, the vice-principal, took hold of her elbow and began to propel her toward the front door. Because she was trying not to raise her arm, her yellow pad was protruding precariously from its place atop her stacks of books. She nudged it with her chin.

"Are you in good voice this morning?" Mr. Singleton asked. "I've excused you from Mr. Litke's homeroom so we can get the mike adjusted."

Instead of answering, Val struggled to find a solution to her dilemma. Glancing down at the legal pad, she thought of the twins' mother, Tatiana, and wished that she, too, were in a Trappist monastery where speech was forbidden. Wait. That was it. From this moment until she reached her own home, she'd observe a vow of silence.

Smiling, she reached for a notepad. As she did, some of her books slid to the pavement. She left them there, but, freeing her elbow, she wrote, "I'VE LOST MY VOICE."

"Is this a joke?" Mr. Singleton said.

Valerie shook her head. She opened her mouth, straining the cords in her neck but making sure no sound came out.

"If this isn't a joke, maybe you should go to the teachers' lounge and gargle with salt water."

"I TRIED THAT."

Mr. Singleton rubbed at his bald head.

Valerie frowned. "CANCEL," she penciled on the paper. She was gathering up her books when she caught sight of Jo and several of her classmates who'd been at

Open Sesame. They seemed to be whispering and pointing in her direction. Were they talking about how she'd acted at the bookstore or about how she looked dressed in black and with her father's hat on her head? Well, let them make fun of her. Like other writers, she'd have to learn to deal with criticism. When she published her new novel with Sverdrup & Liebson, people would make comments about that, too.

Mr. Singleton was talking to her. He had her elbow again and was guiding her into school and down the hall toward the library. The door of the library and the glass windows that faced onto the hall were papered with copies of the book jacket of *The Magic Butter Churn*, and with a set of proofs that Molly Moore had sent from New York. Valerie would have liked to peel them off and hide them.

At that moment Mr. Litke, her English teacher—the one who thought that there hadn't been any truly gifted writers since Charlotte Brontë and Charles Dickens—appeared. Then he and Mr. Singleton and Mrs. Preiss, the librarian, whom the students had nicknamed Miss Priss, began to work on Valerie.

"Take a deep breath. That's right. Just breathe deeply."

"This is simply stage fright."

"Don't worry—you'll feel fine when you get up there."

Val kept angling the notepad that said "CANCEL" in front of them, but they ignored it. If she faltered, Miss Priss would be next to her on the podium to offer encouragement.

Shuddering, Valerie printed another message on the pad. "REST ROOM?"

Mr. Singleton and Mr. Litke frowned, but Miss Priss nodded. "Of course. Just be sure to hurry right back."

She intended to hurry, but back was not the direction she intended to take. Home was more like it. She strode down the hall, moving as quickly as she could without being stopped by a monitor. Now she knew how prison escapees felt when, although fleeing, they tried not to attract attention to themselves. Surely she was the only student at Horton dressed in black with a man's felt hat on her head. Here this outfit was as conspicuous as a prisoner's uniform.

She wheeled around the corner. The front door was in sight. As soon as she had slipped past it, she'd break into a run.

Just then, however, she heard someone behind her, calling her name.

Pausing, she turned her head. It was Jo Samuels entangled with the same knot of her classmates. "Did you really lose your voice? Is Miss Priss really going to read for you? But, Val, assembly's right after homeroom. Where *are* you going?"

Val hunched her shoulders and continued to head toward the front door. Not a word was going to pass her lips.

"She hasn't really lost her voice," someone scoffed.

"Maybe the cat's got her tongue."

Raising one hand in a meaningless gesture, Valerie sent a pleading look in Jo's direction, but Jo shook her head. "What's the matter—aren't we good enough for you anymore?"

Jo's question seemed to set off the others again.

"She hasn't lost her voice. She's just chicken," someone suggested. "She doesn't want us to hear more

28

about the bald prince—the one who used to be a *bad* prince. She's afraid we'll laugh at the prince's hundred bald soldiers and the river of butter. Well, we won't, because now we've got this."

Valerie eyed the door. The bell was ringing, and she only had another twenty yards to go.

" 'Then,' " a falsetto voice sang out, rising above the din, " 'Saralinda pulled up her petticoat and examined the livid purple scar crayoned along the edge of her breastbone. A moment later, she was convulsed with bitter sobs and moaning for her lost . . .' "

As Valerie lurched to a stop, she looked down. Her yellow tablet. She'd dropped it before and had been too busy scribbling on her notepad to realize she'd never retrieved it. Now *they* had the text of her novel.

" 'Crayoned along the edge of her breastbone.' What does that mean? I'd rather hear about a bald prince."

Wheeling, Valerie pulled herself up to her full height and descended on them. She was mortified. Her words, when read aloud, sounded so silly. She snatched the tablet from their hands. Then, still aware of her vow of silence, she stormed away.

"Val," Jo called out. "Wait. Listen—the side of your sweater is all ripped. We can see your—well . . . your breastbone."

Valerie pushed at the front door. Loyalty—where was Jo's loyalty? Val would never speak to her again.

"What does Valerie care?" some boy croaked. "She's above it all. She's cool. Really cool."

"Hey, Val, what's gotten into you?" Jo asked. "You never used to act like this."

"But now she just thinks she's *so* great."

Suddenly, unable to bear it any longer, Valerie turned

back, only dimly aware that she was about to be expelled from the Trappist order. "Why are you being this way? What have I done to you? Am I such a terrible person? Look, I've got things on my mind."

With her chin propped in her hands, Val was shut in her room waiting for the day to be over. She'd behaved so miserably at school, she'd never be able to straighten things out there. Then, once she arrived home, she'd done nothing but sit and stare at the newspaper photo of Stan, Claire, Tekla, and herself, which she'd pulled off the refrigerator and placed on top of her desk. Something about the picture kept nagging at her. Why did she look more like Tekla than like either of her parents?

After a while, aware of an ache in her chest, she went out to the hall, reached for the phone, and dialed.

"T.J.?" she asked, when she heard the husky, familiar voice at the other end.

"Who is this?" Tekla Reis asked.

"Me, Valerie. I need to talk to you."

"About what?"

Valerie examined the torn seam of Claire's sweater. "There's something I've got to ask you."

"Not now," Tekla told her.

"What?"

"I'm busy. Call me back tonight. Around eight."

"But this is important."

"I'm sorry. Really sorry, but we'll have to speak later."

Before Valerie could protest, the line went dead. For several minutes she sat there, wondering how Tekla could have dismissed her in such an unfeeling way.

Then, anxious to do something to comfort herself, she looked up another number and dialed. After a short pause and delicate negotiations with an ill-tempered secretary, she had Molly Moore on the line.

"I'm working on a new novel," she said, speaking up to make sure her voice carried from one coast to the other.

"That's nice," Molly said, her voice partially obscured by a clicking sound.

"It's about twins, stolen from their royal mother and raised by commoners."

"Interesting."

Valerie spoke a little louder. "You do want to do another book of mine, don't you?"

"Yes . . ."

"But, Molly, did you make changes in my story? Was the prince always bald? Was the river always butter?"

"No improvements were made without your approval. And you don't have to shout. I'm not deaf."

"Then what's that noise?"

"My computer. Listen, I can't hang on the phone now."

So Jo was right. Somehow, while Valerie hadn't been paying attention, Molly Moore had managed to make suggestions that altered the original story. Well, it wouldn't happen again. "Listen—about my new manuscript?"

"A new manuscript? Mmm. We'll talk. Okay?"

It was not okay, but Molly Moore was gone, too. Val peered into the mirror over the phone. She was still wearing her father's hat. And something about the newspaper clipping was still bothering her. She growled and pushed the hat back on her head.

from the chair. One elbow jackknifed out from her side, sending a stack of books thudding to the floor.

"Steady there," Val's father said, his voice echoing from somewhere behind Valerie's head. But his gesture of support had come too late.

"This is awful. Horrible. Embarrassing. It's not fair."

"Destroy this tape. Dig a hole," Bennett shouted, interrupting her as she paused for breath.

The next breath she took was in the windowless back room of the bookstore. Her mother was cradling her head and swabbing her face with a wet paper towel. Her father was offering water, while Hatch massaged her fingertips.

"It's going to be all right. All right," her mother murmured. "Don't worry. It's okay. Shhh. Hush. You're fine. Just fine."

By the next morning, when Val was slumped over a bowl of bran flakes examining the "People" section of the paper, the book-signing party had begun to reduce itself to a blur. The article, however, and its headline—*Young Author Churns Out an Epic*—brought everything flooding back. Directly below the headline was the photograph, with her mother's face wary and her father's appearing to be bruised. Valerie had one hand up as if she were about to pick her nose. The Laura Ashley dress, with its lace collar, hung from her shoulders like a frumpy nightgown. To make matters worse, her curly hair was standing out as if she'd inserted one finger in a light socket, and the copy of *The Magic Butter Churn* seemed to be upside down. Meanwhile, in the midst of this scene, Tekla had somehow remained dignified and held herself apart from the Meyerson family, as if

As she was staring into the mirror, it came to her. The truth. She didn't just happen to look like Tekla Reis. There was a reason. She looked like Tekla because T.J. was her mother. Tekla, pregnant yet unmarried, had given Stan and Claire her baby to raise. Then, later, they'd argued over Val, and that's why they were no longer friends.

While Valerie was struggling to assimilate this thought, the doorbell rang. She sprang forward. It was Tekla, she knew, appearing in person to find out why she'd been so distraught. Her real mother wouldn't abandon her when she was in need.

When Val pulled the door open, however, it wasn't Tekla standing there, but her blond, toothy cousin Bennett.

"You going to a funeral?" he asked.

She clenched her teeth. Bennett always made her think of quicksand and trampolines with no safety mats beside them. "Is that what you asked Kate when you brought her to my book-signing party?"

"The redhead with the scar across her cheek? Black was great on her. But you—you look like a refugee who hasn't had a nourishing meal in a year and a half. Or a scarecrow. Or a stand-in for Charlie Chaplin. It's good you decided to copy her clothing instead of her three-inch scar. And, by the way, her name isn't Kate. It's Keaton."

Valerie glared at him. She didn't want to discuss Keaton. Nor was she interested in finding out what Bennett was doing on her doorstep. She had more important things to think about.

"Don't give me that squinty-eyed look," Bennett protested. "I'm only here because your mom called my mom, who sent me, because your school called to see why you'd played hooky. I'm supposed to make sure you're at home."

"Well, I am. So you can go."

"What's with you, Val? Ever since this book came out, you've been acting like you expect everyone to clap and call out 'Author! Author!' But that doesn't happen in real life. Only in the theater, and it hardly ever happens there anymore."

Adjusting the brim of her hat, Valerie sighed. Her long, thin body was just like Tekla's. Her elongated chin. Her dark hair, too. Maybe Stan and Claire hadn't just argued with Tekla. Maybe they'd gone to court to keep from losing custody of her.

"Go away," she begged. "I don't have time for this now."

" 'Author! Author!' " Bennett said, managing to sound like a barking seal.

Unable to deal with him one minute longer, Valerie took hold of the door and slammed it in his face.

# 4

*As Saralinda drew her cape around her shoulders and burrowed into the haystack to escape the mist, she thought of Margolite and of her real parents, praying that the kind peasants who had raised her would come to understand the depth of her need to have . . .*

". . . a black skirt and sweater?" Claire asked. "Is that what we're after? And another pair of black jeans?"

Valerie nodded absentmindedly as she picked apart the BLT sandwich and began to eat the bacon out of the middle. Clothing didn't seem important just now. What really concerned her was finding out the truth about Tekla and her parents.

Claire leaned forward. "I remember how it was when I was your age. One day I woke up and decided all my clothes were too babyish."

As Claire was speaking, Val gazed at her across the table in the Neiman-Marcus rotunda. Claire's round face with its green eyes and freckles was attractive, but it did appear to be the face of someone to whom Val wasn't biologically related. Thinking about that possibility made Val feel sad.

"What's wrong?" Claire asked.

Valerie raised the Borsalino so it didn't cut off the circulation in the tops of her ears. "Who says there's something wrong?"

After asking the waitress for the check, Claire turned back toward Valerie. "I do. Your father does. Look, every morning we have to plead with you to go to school. You've suddenly quit the swim team and decided that black is your favorite color. Then you shut yourself in your room and write, but every time Dad or I appear, you shove your pad into a drawer as if it contains top-secret, classified information." Claire paused. "Do you want me to go on?"

Valerie shook her head. She loved her mother and felt guilty about the way she'd been acting.

Claire put a twenty-dollar bill and some change on the table. Then she rose to her feet. "We know your book has been a disappointment. Being published has not been as wonderful as you anticipated. But that's not all. What is it, Ducky?"

Val stood up and followed Claire out of the restaurant. Then, one after the other, they stepped onto the down escalator. "I feel . . ." Val said to the back of Claire's head as they were walking off it at street level, "as though there are important things you and Dad aren't telling me."

"Like what?"

When Claire stopped to readjust the buckled strap of her shoulder bag, Valerie edged toward one of the cosmetic counters. She didn't know where to begin or how to avoid being hurtful. Claire was a good person, a caring parent, yet Val felt compelled to speak. Pausing, she rotated a bin of sample eye shadows.

Claire reached out and steadied the display. She peered into its horizontal mirror. "I look so washed out, so mousy."

Val nodded. Claire was right, but if she learned how to apply cosmetics it might make a difference. Besides, thinking about how Claire looked was easier than probing to discover whether Tekla was her biological mother. Turning, Val reexamined Claire. If she stopped wearing floppy bow ties, that might help, too. Many people at the bank had been fired recently, and Valerie thought that Claire was worried that if she untied the bow, her head would roll. "Maybe you should have a make-over."

"Huh?"

"You know," Val answered, trying to squeeze all thoughts about Tekla out of her consciousness, "let one of the women here do your face and show you what products are best for your skin. You could make yourself more dramatic."

"Would I really look better? Or is this a diversionary tactic? Come on, what's bothering you? Out with it."

Val peered into a tray displaying three shades of peach-colored powder. "Tekla Reis," she said, dismayed to find that she was unable to discipline either her mind or her tongue. "Tell me about when you and she and Dad used to be friends. And why you're not anymore. What happened? Has she ever been married? And if not, why not? Do I look like her? I do, don't I?"

"You look like my sister," Claire said, tapping at the elbow of one of the blue-smocked saleswomen.

"Me?" the saleswoman asked.

"No, she—my daughter here—looks like my sister and like her son, Bennett, too. They have the same high foreheads and elongated chins. But her height comes from her father's side of the family. He has tall uncles."

"We have a make-over special today," the saleswoman said.

Claire smiled at her. Then, turning toward Val, she shook her head. "No, Tekla's never been married."

Val stood there waiting for her to say more.

But Claire was seating herself on a stool, being draped, and having colorless moisturizer rubbed into her face. The rest of Val's questions were not about to be answered. Well, what had she expected? That Claire would stand in the middle of Neiman-Marcus and confess that she and Stan had adopted Tekla Reis's child?

Just then something startling occurred to Valerie. Maybe Tekla had been a surrogate mother and her father, through artificial insemination, was Stan Meyerson. The papers were full of stories about surrogate mothers. After all of Claire's four-month and five-month miscarriages, maybe she and Stan had asked T.J. to have a baby for them. That would explain everything. Especially if Tekla had changed her mind about giving up Valerie and fought for her in court.

Most adopted children were told from the time that they could talk that they were "chosen children." Being a surrogate child, whose parents had battled over her in court, was much more complex. If that were the case, Val could understand why Stan and Claire had wanted to protect her as long as possible. But she was old enough now.

Val examined Claire's face. It was covered with red

dots, making her look as if she had some rare and possibly fatal strain of measles. As Valerie stood there, the smocked woman began, with circular motions, to blend the substance into Claire's skin with the tips of her fingers.

"Hiding the truth from me isn't going to do any of us any good," Val stated, opening a sample lipstick and using it to make a streak on the back of her hand.

"Are we still talking about Tekla?" her mother asked. "Because, if we are, there's really not much to say. She and Dad knew each other when they were in graduate school and, afterward, out here—the three of us were friends—for a while. Then we drifted apart. If you want to know any more, maybe you should ask Tekla."

The cosmetic woman had begun to brush purple streaks over Claire's eyes. She was also vying with Val for Claire's attention. She wanted to discuss what products should be purchased to duplicate the effect of the make-over. While they conversed, Val rubbed some sample blush and eye color onto her own face. She highlighted her mouth with dark plummy lipstick.

By the time Claire was staring into the hand mirror at the final effect of the woman's handiwork, Valerie hardly recognized her. Even with the silk bow curling under her chin, Claire looked beautiful and sophisticated.

"What will Dad think?" Val asked.

"Dad," Claire told her, as soon as she had finished up with the smocked woman, "will never know."

Only a few moments later, Valerie and her mother were up at the rest-room sinks. Claire was scrubbing her face. Streaks of purple and pink coloring were running down her face and dribbling onto her white shirt.

"But you were so glamorous that way," Valerie moaned.

"Like some kind of hooker," Claire mumbled, bending closer to the mirror and using a soggy Kleenex to wipe eyeliner off her eyes. "With my luck, I'd run into my boss or his boss on the way to the garage. This was a terrible idea. What got into me?"

"You didn't want to tell me about Tekla," Val said.

Claire's head jerked up. Her newly washed cheeks and forehead seemed to stiffen and take on the pale cold tint of a glazed ceramic mask. She squinted. "Oh, no, Val. It's on your face, too. When did you do that? Here. Take a towel and wipe it off. You're too young for all of this. I told your father, pleaded with him. I knew it was a mistake."

Valerie should have been relieved that Claire let her remove the makeup herself. Not too long ago, she would have mortified Val by spitting on a towel and sliming her like a mother cat grooming a kitten. Val swabbed at her face until it stung from the stiffness of the waffled paper and she'd managed to smudge pink grease under the brim of the hat.

"Get that spot next to your nose," her mother said, as she used a dusty shade of lipstick to daub her mouth back into an oversize Cheerio. "Then we have to get going. We've still got all our shopping to do."

Valerie scrubbed at the offending blob. "I don't feel like it. Let's just go home."

"I'd really like to get you some of the things we talked about."

"Not today."

"First you needed stuff desperately. Now you don't

feel like it. I could have been in my office, catching up. But I thought we'd spend a nice Saturday together. And then—without explanation—you've changed your mind. I may be good-natured, but I'm not that good-natured."

"Don't get angry," Val pleaded, leaning down and nuzzling Claire's shoulder apologetically. "I'll come next week. By myself. If you want, I'll even use the advance money from *The Magic Butter Churn*."

Claire stepped backward. "You'd spend your advance money on jeans? Are you serious? Yes, you are. Maybe I'm too old to have a child your age. Yes, that's it. These days, I seem to have one thing after another nipping at my heels."

She paused and shook her head. "Books. Makeovers. Advance money. Whatever I do, someone is micromanaging me. I'm forty-eight years old, and my life is being run by a bank with a heart of ice and a twelve-year-old whose body is raging with hormones."

Stepping forward, Val reached out toward her mother. "Mom, are you all right?"

"Of course I'm all right."

People in the rest room edged away from them. Claire had not raised her voice, but she had enunciated each word emphatically. A woman in a red suit left without washing her hands. Someone else stayed locked in a cubicle, as if afraid to come out and find herself in the middle of a combat zone.

Valerie frowned. This was as close as Claire ever came to losing her temper. In fact, her normal body temperature seemed to be no higher than ninety-three degrees. But she wasn't cool now. Val lowered her eyes and stared at the tops of her white sneakers, trying to remember exactly what Claire had just said. Tekla had said she should pay attention and use her own experience.

Well, that was what she was trying to do. The fact that her mother had gotten so rattled over so little convinced Valerie even more that she had begun to unravel the clues to the mystery of her life. She was Tekla's daughter and her father's. That much was clear. What she still had to discover was the details. What had happened? How had they persuaded T.J. to be a surrogate mother for them?

As Valerie was attempting to sort out these matters, Claire took a deep breath and shoved her hands into the pockets of her green velours skirt. Her face looked calm, but her taut fists made her pockets look as if they were weighted down with doorknobs.

When she spoke again, however, her tone was normal. "We're running out of time, and, besides, my feet are in terrible shape—sending pains up the back of my calves."

Val tilted her head to one side. "Does menopause do that?"

The minute the words were out of her mouth, she knew she'd made a mistake. She should not have said that. What had gotten into her?

But this time, Claire seemed armed for her question and barely blinked in response. "What? Oh, never mind. I heard you the first time. But come on, let's get moving. And don't argue with me. Because, like it or not, we're going to do what we came here for. Now. Because your dad is expecting us back by four." She turned toward the door. Then, hesitating for an instant, she looked back in Valerie's direction. "By the way, for your information, I am not yet menopausal."

Valerie heard what sounded like a swarm of angry bees heading down the hallway toward her room. But it wasn't bees, she realized, only the sound of Stan's electric razor.

"May I come in, Ducky?" His question and his knock were simultaneous with the opening of her door.

Leaning back against the headboard of her bed, Valerie pressed the yellow tablet to her chest. "There's not much privacy around here," she said.

Reaching down, she slid the tablet under the bed. Then she flicked out one hand and shoved the various pieces of black clothing Claire had bought for her to one side. "Sit down."

Stan turned off the razor. "I'll stand."

Valerie bit down on her bottom lip. Her father never came into her room without seating himself at the foot of the bed and wrapping one arm around the end post. "What's wrong?"

"I'd ask you the same thing, only I gather your mother already has. So, instead of asking, I thought I'd just say a couple of things. Bruno Bettelheim—you've heard me mention his name before?"

Val nodded. "The doctor from Chicago—the fairy-tale one who studied kids?"

"Right. The very same. Well, he said we should evaluate children by their behavior at home, in school, and in the neighborhood. If they're doing all right in two out of three of these, he said not to worry. But here you are—problems at school, problems in the neighborhood. Isn't slamming the door in Bennett's face a symptom of distress? And now you seem determined to alienate your mom and me."

"But I didn't even want all this stuff," Val said. "Mom insisted. She was completely out of control. Not only a skirt and jeans, but a tunic, a scarf, leggings, tights, sneakers." As Val spoke, she scanned her father's face, trying to decide if her nose, although more pointed, wasn't similar to his. It was hard to tell, because he was so fair-skinned and his nose was partially obscured by the bushy mustache that grew beneath it. Today he appeared almost albino with the overhead light spilling down on his shock of silvery blond hair. No, they weren't very much alike, but maybe as she got older she'd look less like Tekla and more like him.

"Valerie, don't space out just now. Please."

"I'm sorry," she mumbled. "I'll listen."

He rotated the electric razor in his hands and examined it for a moment. Then he looked up at her again. "Well, all I'm saying is that your mom and I feel you're not behaving very skillfully. And we think efforts should be made to remedy that."

Val nodded her head.

"Your mom feels you've developed some sort of obsession about Tekla. Like this business about wearing black."

Standing up, Valerie walked over to her dresser. She picked up the Borsalino and settled it on top of her head. She could see herself in the mirror and her father's reflection behind her. "Tekla doesn't wear black," she said.

When he didn't answer, she turned around. Looking uneasy, he backed up, jarring the switch on his razor again and releasing the swarm of bees into the middle of her room. "No," he said, fumbling to turn it off, "I guess she doesn't. It's yellow she likes. The damnedest shade of chrome yellow."

As he was speaking, she was suddenly aware that Claire, a grim expression on her face, was standing in the doorway.

Valerie, off balance, watched her father shuffle his feet and turn toward her. They might as well be honest and tell her the truth, because she was going to keep probing.

"Don't. Not now, honey," Claire said, addressing Stan pleadingly. "You're not feeling well. Another time? All right?"

It was not all right with Valerie. She wanted everything in the open. "No way," she protested. "Let's talk now."

"But, Val—oh, Val, please."

The intensity in her mother's voice made Val reconsider. "Well, if we don't talk now, soon. Very soon. Because I'm not giving up. I plan to observe and be ruthless."

Stan frowned. "What?"

"What is she talking about?" Claire asked Stan. " 'To observe and be ruthless'? Do we know any twelve-year-olds who talk like that?"

Her father's face twitched and brightened. In fact, he seemed suddenly amused.

Humming, he walked forward and buzzed Claire with his razor.

" 'You are my sunshine,' " he began to sing, " 'my only sunshine. You make me happy when skies are gray . . .' Somehow, somewhere, my love, I detect the fine hand—or, rather, the fine tongue—of our friend T.J."

# 5

*The wine cellar was damp and echoed with the ominous clicking sound of rats' toenails. Tatiana wanted to scream, but a strange man's lips were pressed against hers, sucking the breath from her body. If she ever got out of here alive, she vowed that the first thing she'd do was . . .*

"Sunbathe without a top? Why not? It's splendid. Makes you feel so free."

Tekla Reis was speaking. She and Valerie were standing at the kitchen window of Tekla's narrow redwood house, looking down on the secluded deck below. The sunbather was Tekla's friend, Lenore, who lived in the studio apartment on the ground floor of the house.

Lenore's breasts were large, firm globes. She was tilted to the left, and they were, too. Valerie, embarrassed to be staring at Lenore while she was asleep, turned away and began to examine the beamed ceiling above her head. Not that she cared about it or about the rest of the house. She'd come to T.J.'s hoping to obtain the answers that she hadn't been able to get at home.

But, uncertain how to proceed, she let her eye canvass the house. Its two-story living room was strewn with jewel-toned rugs, old furniture, and an assortment of brass and copper cooking pots that needed polishing. On the coffee table in front of the fireplace was an oversize marble foot. Tekla said it was a saint's foot that her grandfather had stolen from some English cathedral where he'd found it already broken off.

"Shouldn't you try and return it?" Val asked.

Tekla turned away from the window, crossed the room, and pushed an accumulation of papers off the couch. Then she sat down. "It's been sixty years since he picked it up. We'd have to lug it back and try it on every crippled saint in the realm. But that's not why you dropped in this afternoon. What's percolating in that fertile mind of yours?"

Even though Tekla had asked, Val felt too startled to tell her the truth. She shrugged. "I came to ask if you wanted to go swimming."

Valerie, because she had quit the swim team, hadn't been to the pool in several weeks, so she hadn't seen Tekla at all. Nor, after T.J. had been so remote the last time she'd phoned, had Val been willing to call again. Instead, she'd stopped by on a Saturday afternoon as if Tekla's house in the alley on Russian Hill were in her neighborhood and not three bus transfers away from her home.

Tekla closed her eyes. "Please don't make me go swimming. I loathe it."

"But you swim all the time. You've been swimming all your life."

Opening one eye, Tekla squinted in her direction. "Did I ever say that?"

"No."

Valerie tried to remember what T.J. might have said about why she swam. Chances are Val had never asked her.

"I did compete in high school. But until last April I hadn't been—except involuntarily—in a pool in twenty years. There. I've confessed. Now you know."

Val seated herself in the straight-backed needlepoint chair next to the fireplace. No sooner had she done so than Khan, Tekla's silver Persian, sprang from the shadows onto her lap. Khan burrowed with his front paws and rolled, creating a Milky Way of gleaming hair across Val's dark clothing. Then he was gone.

Brushing ineffectually at the shed fur, Valerie knew that she no longer needed to ask why Tekla had been at Rossi Pool. The answer was obvious. She'd been swimming there because it was the only way she knew to meet her daughter, Val, and begin to get to know her.

"T.J.?"

"Hmm?"

Val leaned forward. "I need to ask you something."

"Oh, look at you. You're so intense. So bright-eyed and bushy-tailed. I remember how it felt. I miss it." Tekla drew her knees up next to her chest and wrapped her arms around them. "Sure. Whatever. Ask me anything."

Suddenly Valerie felt panicky. The question she found herself asking was different from the one she had meant to pose. "Do twins run in your family?"

Tekla stared up at the ceiling. "Damn, I've got to find some way to cut that frigging ivy. It's coming through the roof and is going to cause a leak. No, there are no twins in my family. And anyway, we're each so difficult, I think that any Reis who had twins would probably drown one at birth rather than try to raise a pair of them. Oh, don't look at me that way. I was just kidding."

Nodding, Valerie raised her eyes and noticed that tendrils of ivy were growing between the beams of the ceiling. As she was wondering how anyone could get up there to clip them, she realized that she wasn't a twin. The lost twin had been only a figment of her imagination. She should stick to sleuthing out the facts about her birth that were real.

She edged her chair closer to the couch where Tekla lay. "What about being a surrogate mother? Would you do that?"

"For money?"

"For any reason."

"That's a good question. Food for thought. Hmm. Certainly not for money. But—well . . . would I, Lenny?"

Lenore was leaning against the archway leading from the kitchen. Not only was she interrupting a private discussion, but she was still wearing nothing except a pair of white cotton gym shorts. Her seminude appearance made Val uncomfortable. She didn't know how to talk to Lenore without acknowledging the presence of her breasts.

Using a thumb and forefinger as a pincer, Valerie began to remove silver cat hairs from her jeans. Tekla hadn't said she would be a surrogate mother, but she hadn't said she wouldn't be one. Although Val felt as if she was getting closer to the truth, she was inclined to proceed slowly. Uncovering the mystery of her past was like doing a jigsaw puzzle. If the pieces fitted together too easily, there'd be no satisfaction to doing it. Val was finding the process of discovery pleasurable. She'd wondered why Tekla had never married, and now she found herself trying to figure out if Lenore Baker had anything to do with that. Lenny had rented the apartment in T.J.'s house for years. They were both writers, both unmarried, and both seemed to have the same group of friends. Maybe there was some kind of special relationship between them.

"Hey, Lenny, you can put on your shirt now," Tekla said. "The *Playboy* photographer just called to say he can't come today."

The two women exchanged looks and chuckled.

Lenny pulled a shawl off a chair and draped it over her shoulders. Then she sidled up behind Val. "How's your writing coming, Little Author? What're your sales figures? Is your book doing well?"

Reacting instinctively, Valerie hunched her shoulders. Lenore must have been the kind of child that tore legs off beetles and wings off butterflies. Val didn't know how her book was coming. Even if she was able to get Molly Moore on the phone, Molly seemed reluctant to say how many copies of *Butter Churn* had been sold. It made Val uncomfortable when Lenore, who was shorter than she, patronized her by calling her little. Still, if she and Tekla were friends and Tekla was Val's mother, she should learn to accept her.

"I'm not too interested in that book anymore," she told Lenore. "It's not very good. But I have started to work on a new one."

"Like Judith," Lenore commented, speaking to Tekla. Then she turned back toward Val. "We have a weaver friend who always says the only thing that interests her is what she has on the loom. How sophisticated you are to have come to that conclusion at your tender age. So tell me, what are you writing about?"

"My life," Valerie said.

"Is there any sex in it?"

"Well . . . yes," she admitted reluctantly.

Lenore ran her fingers through her graying blond hair. "Your life and your sexual experiences. Very admirable. Any manuscripts you'd like to show me?" Lenore, in addition to writing short stories, edited a literary magazine.

Instead of waiting for Val to answer, Lenore continued. "You see, T, this young woman has intellectual honesty. She's not hiding, feinting, ducking the truth."

Something important was going on. Lenore was speaking to Tekla in some kind of code while Tekla was rising from the couch and crossing to one corner of the room, where she began to rifle through the contents of an old trunk. What, Val wondered, was she going to produce? A tiny sweater and a pair of booties that Valerie had worn when she was first born?

No, it wasn't baby garments after all. What Tekla was holding was a mesh bag bulging with wooden balls. "We've been liberated," she told Lenore. "I've confessed, so we don't have to swim anymore. So what about having dinner and then going lawn-bowling? We haven't done that in an age."

The object of the game, Lenore and T.J. had explained as they were eating dinner at a restaurant called Ciao, was to roll one's green or red balls as close as possible to the small blond wood one. The only problem was that this was a game for two people or four people but not for three.

Valerie was happy that Stan and Claire had agreed to let her spend the evening with Tekla and Lenore but puzzled by the fact that they were devoting the time to what seemed to be a stupid game played under even more stupid conditions. In the rapidly diminishing light, the small ball was a blur on the grass of the pocket park across from Ciao and the other eight were so dark they were hardly visible at all. The streetlamps, instead of improving the vision, merely created glary, overlapping pools of light.

Valerie couldn't help imagining what Stan and Claire might say if they were present. Valerie felt as if one of them were peering over each shoulder, whispering in her ears, questioning her. This was hardly what they would call a productive activity. It didn't improve cardiovascular function, make money, or prepare one to face the future in any way she could discern. Nor did it feel safe to be in a deserted park at night.

"Remember you live in a city, and behave accordingly," her parents always reminded her. "Move purposefully. Never loiter."

Valerie knew that what she and Tekla and Lenore were doing was not purposeful, but she did want to get to know Tekla better.

Still, Stan and Claire continued to alarm her by whispering in her ears. They were particularly wary of street people. On a bench about ten feet away was a disheveled homeless woman whose belongings were layered on top of a child's red wagon she'd parked by her feet. What would keep her from rising up and attacking the three of them with a butcher knife?

As Valerie was about to take hold of the sleeve of Tekla's yellow sweatshirt and suggest that they bowl someplace else, Tekla beckoned to the woman. "Would you like to play? We need a fourth."

"Me?" the woman asked in a whiny tone. As she spoke, she was fumbling with the buttons of a sweater she wore under a jacket that was so short and tight that her upper arms seemed splinted at an angle away from her sides.

"Yes, of course," T said. "Come on. I saw you watching. I know you'd like to join us."

A few moments later, Val and Tekla were bowling with the red balls teamed up against Lenore and the woman, who told them that her name was Fred.

Fred and Tekla and Lenore were talking and joking as they rolled the balls past Fred's wagon, but Valerie felt uncomfortable. Whenever she got too close to Fred, she was aware that the woman smelled of perspiration, of gin, or of both. Fred's hair was cropped close to her head. She'd probably done that with her knife, Val reasoned nervously, yet when the woman smiled, her teeth were white and even.

Flashing these white teeth in Val's direction, she took a step toward her. "I wish I knew where my mother was," she whined, tugging at Val's sweatshirt. "Did anyone ever tell you how much you look like yours?"

"My what?"

"Your mother."

Valerie wanted to jerk her arm away, but she hesitated, unwilling to be rude. Fred had, after all, reached a conclusion in an instant that had taken her much longer. With raised eyebrows, Tekla and Lenore were acknowledging they'd heard the question. When neither of them contradicted Fred, Val didn't either. In fact, she took a deep breath and began to relax. What they were doing was interesting and unusual. No member of the Meyerson family would ever lawn-bowl at night with a street person. Even Bennett, if he'd happened upon her, would have gazed at her superciliously, but the longer the four of them bowled, the more natural it seemed.

Fred was handicapped by her short, straitjacket sleeves, but she squinted and rolled each ball carefully. "Mothers are a good thing," she muttered after a while, speaking to no one in particular. "But bunions are not."

"Yes," Val answered.

Suddenly aware that she was fortunate enough to have two mothers—an unorthodox one and a conventional one, a surrogate mother and an adoptive one—she felt pity for Fred. Fred, too, had been someone's sweet infant, yet was now alone, living on the streets.

As if Tekla were reading Val's mind, she squinted through the darkness and asked Fred, "What about surrogacy? Being a surrogate mother? You ever think of that? Val raised the question today, and it's an interesting one."

"Have a kid for someone else?" Fred asked. "Is there money in that?"

Lenore dropped to her knees to measure how close the balls were. "Ten thousand dollars. Fifteen, if you're lucky."

Fred gulped. "Ten grand. Whew. Then why am I doing what I'm doing?"

"I don't know. Why are you?" Tekla demanded.

"Your voice is changing. How come?" Lenore asked. "What happened to your whine?"

"Don't. Stop," Val said, aware that she had begun to feel protective of Fred. Why were T.J. and Lenore turning on the woman and attacking her? Val had been about to ask Tekla how she'd feel about offering Fred a bath and a bed for the night.

"Damn," Fred said. "And I thought I was doing such a good job. How did you catch on?"

Valerie looked from side to side. Fred seemed younger than she had a few minutes ago and her posture was better, but this made Val feel more confused. Instead of saying anything, she stood there, waiting for the situation to become less murky.

"Your nails are filed," Tekla said. "Your shoes fit."

"You have gold crowns on your molars. The wagon's too shiny. And what did you do with the gin? Daub it on all your pulse points, like perfume?"

Finally Val couldn't stand it any longer. "What's going on?" she pleaded.

No one answered.

Instead, the three women looked at one another and began to chuckle. "We're writers," Lenore told Fred, as if that was in and of itself some kind of explanation. "Details are our bread and butter."

"Also our excuse for being the way we are," Tekla added. "What's yours?"

Fred began to peel herself out of the constraining jacket. "Actress," she said. "Trying to get some life experience."

"Just like our daughter here," Tekla commented. "She, too, is accumulating life experiences as rapidly as possible. Watch out. She'll probably write about you, and you may not like what she says. That's the sorry price of fame, Fred."

"Laura," the woman who had previously called herself Fred offered. As she was saying her real name, she stepped closer to Tekla. "Hey, wait. I know you. You came to Stanford and spoke to one of my English classes. You read us a long poem about two women in a forest."

"*Titania's Revenge,*" Tekla muttered.

"So you are Tekla Reis. But you haven't published anything in years. What's happened to you?"

"I used to be Tekla Reis. Now I seem to be someone else. I don't know what happened. People. Events. Or maybe I just need a new agent."

"A little intellectual honesty would be nice," Lenore suggested. "And courage to face—"

"Don't hock at me. I'm not feeling very strong," Tekla said. "Please, lay off."

No, don't, Valerie wanted to shout, keep talking. Tell me more.

Tekla, however, had turned her back on them. Stooping down, she was gathering up the wooden balls and thunking them into their orange mesh bag.

# 6

*As Saralinda knelt before the gravestone, her tears mingled with the falling raindrops. She was crying, because she'd come too late and because her twin, Margolite, had faced death alone. If only her mother was with her at this moment, the two of them would be . . .*

"Getting ready to leave for Aunt DeDe and Uncle Stuart's? Don't be pokey."

Valerie pushed aside her tablet and a half-finished letter to Molly Moore asking why she had so much trouble reaching her and whether she should get an agent. Instead of answering Claire, she stared down at her bare feet, observing the way in which her baby toes curled up over the ones next to them.

Today was her father's birthday, an occasion she usually enjoyed, but this year she'd given it little thought and done nothing except buy him a box of Walgreens pecan turtles.

"Valerie?"

Claire was poised in the doorway, dressed in the new rose-colored knit suit that made her look something like a Polish sausage. "What's going on? We're ready to leave, and you're not even dressed."

"But I am," Val said. "All but my shoes."

"Honey, this is a special occasion. I'd hoped you'd wear something nice. What's wrong with the Laura Ashley?"

"It's raining. And I don't wear flowers anymore."

Claire peered into the mirror over Valerie's dresser, adjusting the bow at her neck and tugging at the knit skirt, trying to make it cling less tightly around her bottom. "It was just a suggestion. We're not going to fight about clothes, are we?"

Standing up, Valerie flipped the Borsalino from the bedpost onto her head. "No."

"Then why're you so sulky? I thought we were over the fuss about the book and things were going better at school."

Suddenly guilty, Val reached out and wrapped an arm over her mother's shoulders. Things were not any better at school. She'd never figured out a way to apologize to her classmates, so she was trying to avoid them instead. In three months, school would be out, and Val would have a whole summer to devise a strategy for dealing with these problems. Three months from now, she also hoped she and her father and Claire and Tekla would no longer have secrets from one another.

Val bent down to nuzzle Claire's cheek. "Everything's fine. Just fine. Where's Dad?"

Claire slid an arm around Valerie's back. "We're so lucky to have you," she mused.

Glancing sideways, Valerie was aware that Claire's hair needed a touch-up and that baby crows had joined the old ones leaving their tracks at the corners of her eyes. Claire seemed more human, approachable. Perhaps this was the time to ask about Tekla.

Val had taken a deep breath when Claire, dropping her arm and moving away, spoke first. "Your dad's feeling rocky today. So we need to take it easy on him."

"Again?" Valerie clenched her fists together. It was always something. If it wasn't bad feet or aching guts, it was calculating the burn, interest rates going south, or deals cratering.

"I'm afraid so. But he's supposed to modify his diet—cut out chocolate and alcohol—and that should help."

"Okay," she said. But her voice was tight, and she knew she was going to have a terrible evening.

"Still playing the duchess, I hear," Bennett commented when he waylaid Valerie in the hallway between the dining room and the kitchen. "Still impressed with yourself?"

To help out her aunt, she was carrying a pewter platter with a ham on it. "I'm really not. Besides, how would you know?"

Bennett spread his arms to prevent her from dodging past him into the dining room. "I have my sources. And some of them also tell me your folks are in the middle of an argument."

"No they're not. It's just my dad's stomach again."

"You fall for that old line? You're such a baby. Something's going on, trust me—something about your book and Tekla Reis's influence on you."

Bennett's sources were none other than his mother, Claire's sister, DeDe, the one whose chin Valerie was supposed to have. DeDe liked to make phone calls from the bathtub, spreading a tidal wave of rumors across

San Francisco. Aunt DeDe, with her glitzy, oversized earrings, was not one of Valerie's favorite people. Uncle Stuart also seemed to salivate over any morsel of gossip. So did Bennett.

Valerie, thinking, licked her lips. "Listen, will you tell me something?"

"Sure. What?"

"My mother—do you remember seeing her pregnant?"

"Of course I remember. Your mother was *always* pregnant." As Bennett spoke, he edged closer and seemed to exude the faint odor of bug spray.

"Stop," she warned. "Don't touch me or I'll—"

"Don't worry. To me, you are about as significant as the hole in a doughnut. So scoot. Get lost. Meander along in your own little solipsistic world where—"

"Cut it out," she cried, offended both by his tone of voice and by his selection of a word she didn't understand.

"Why should I?"

"Because, if you don't, the next time I see you with Keaton, I'll tell her about your Binky. Or about how you peed in your bed until you were ten and used to dress up in your mother's clothes. So lay off, will you?"

As Val was threatening Bennett, she stepped forward. The ham slid sideways, wobbled off the platter, and skidded across the parquet floor. Valerie was lunging for it when her parents and her aunt appeared.

"Ask the maid to get the other ham," Bennett said, quoting an old joke and, at the same time, managing to remove himself from being blamed for the incident.

A few minutes later, pretending for the sake of the family occasion that the scene in the back hall hadn't taken place, Uncle Stuart was carving the ham while Aunt DeDe told them that her hairdresser said that the deputy sheriff who'd been caught in a vice raid was an alcoholic, too.

Valerie, watching and listening, brooded in silence. Not only had Bennett contrived to trap and infuriate her, but he had made her see that her parents did appear to be in the middle of an argument.

Although they were seated side by side, Claire's shoulders were angled away from Stan and toward DeDe. Once Valerie began to pay attention, she realized her parents were addressing the rest of the family members instead of each other.

"He shouldn't be having his baked potato with sour cream, because he's supposed to avoid milk products," Claire told her sister. "And chocolate. And alcohol."

"My wife," Stan informed Uncle Stuart, "has started to think she's my mother. The next thing I know, she'll be cutting my meat."

Valerie lifted a too large wedge of ham on her fork and put it in her mouth. As she listened to the sound of her own labored chewing, she wondered if this disagreement had just started or if it had been going on for weeks. All of a sudden she felt jumpy. Parents, after all, were supposed to be parents. It was their responsibility not to begin acting like people and messing up their children's lives.

Putting down her fork, she gazed at Stan, then at Claire. She felt as if she were observing a pair of strangers. Stan, who'd missed the edge of his chin with his razor, appeared to be the sort of sensitive, somewhat beaten-down, puzzled middle-aged man who might grind his teeth in his sleep at night. His pale eyebrows strained to unite across the permanent furrow down the bridge of his nose. This was a man who worried a lot. His shoulders were slumped.

Claire's were very straight. With her head propped rigidly between them, she looked like an oversized baby doll. Rubber bands were holding her arms and legs in place, and they were twisted too tight. Despite her roundness, everything about Claire was pale and bloodless. Tonight, she seemed particularly ashen and kept clearing her throat in a way Val had never noticed before.

"Oh, Stan," she protested, in a voice that pierced Val's meditations and also her notion that they weren't addressing each other directly. "I don't believe you did that. You know you shouldn't. Why can't you—"

Claire's voice broke off in mid-sentence. As she began to coil the dinner napkin between her hands, Val could see her internal rubber bands tightening, too, bringing back her self-control. Still, Claire looked as if she could use a hug. Stan was leaning toward her now. He was apologizing for whatever he'd done and raising one hand to pat her shoulder. But he didn't offer her the hug she seemed to need.

Valerie lowered her eyes and scanned the table. Then she turned back toward her parents. Somehow, while she'd been observing them, the dinner plates had been removed and smaller ones with slices of birthday cake had appeared. Stan had chocolate crumbs speckling one corner of his mouth, which meant he'd been eating the cake he wasn't supposed to have.

Bennett's chair was scraping against the floor. He was checking his watch, saying it was time for him to pick up Kate.

"Kate?" Val said. "I thought her name was Keaton."

But no one paid any attention to her, because her father was on his feet, and he was talking in a tense, urgent voice. "Listen, I'm sorry, but I need to go now. So, excuse me. Please excuse me, but don't let me break up the party. Just stay where you are, and I'll walk to Market Street and catch the bus."

Valerie pressed the tips of her fingers against the tabletop and made an instantaneous decision.

"I'm going, too," she said, standing up so rapidly that her chair tipped backwards, rattling DeDe's china cabinet. Righting the chair, she retrieved her hat from the sideboard. "It's Daddy's birthday and he shouldn't be alone."

"They didn't even try to stop us from leaving," Valerie said, splashing from the middle of one inky puddle to the middle of another.

"Colitis has few redeeming qualities," her father replied, carefully stepping around the same two puddles. "It's not a socially acceptable illness. And if one has it long enough, sooner or later all one's friends become former friends."

"And one's relatives become former relatives?" Val asked.

"I hope not. But, yes, sometimes they do."

"Why were you and Mom fighting about what you can and can't eat? Isn't that kind of dumb?"

"We weren't fighting about food," her father replied, taking hold of her shoulder and angling her around the corner toward Market Street. "Appearances can be deceiving."

"Then what was it?"

"Sometimes, Ducky, when people are nosy, they end up finding out things they didn't want to know."

Val opened her mouth to ask Stan, again, what *was* really going on, but, suddenly suffused with nervousness, she found herself unable to speak.

It was raining harder now, but she and her father were still ambling along as if it were sunshine pouring down on them. Swallowing hard, Val adjusted the brim of her hat, deflecting the water so it wouldn't drip down her back.

Stan began to walk faster. "Step on it," he urged.

"I am, I am."

"Aren't you going to offer me my hat? It's foul out here. Why did we leave DeDe's anyway?"

"Because you're not feeling well," Val said, lifting off the hat and handing it to him.

A bus was pulling up at the curb. Moving in step, they began to race toward it. They were almost there when the bus driver accelerated, splashing them with muddy gutter water. For a moment they stood shaking their fists after him. Then, at the same time, they both noticed the BART sign. Without hesitating, they headed down the grimy, wet Market Street stairs.

BART, the Bay Area Rapid Transit, was San Francisco's answer to New York's subway. The problem was that it sent trains only to Oakland, Walnut Creek, and suburbs east of the city.

But, at this moment, neither Stan nor Valerie seemed to care. They were out of the rain and stepping aboard a train bound for Concord.

"I'm feeling okay," Stan said, as they began hurtling forward into the tunnel beneath the Bay.

The smell of damp wool permeated the air. Val even

thought she saw steam escaping from their clothing in the heated car. She had her father alone on a ride to nowhere. This was the moment she'd longed for. Now she could ask about Tekla. Still, being alone with Stan, feeling the waves of his intensity rock against her equally intense ones, made her panicky and hesitant.

Sometimes when she gazed at her father, she thought of pyramids and granite cliffs, or warm fires and surefooted polar bears, yet today these images seemed inaccurate. Despite what he'd just said about how he felt, his face was almost as pallid as Claire's, and he did not look like himself. Besides, it was his birthday. Maybe, she told herself anxiously, she should arrange for a dinner together with her parents, Tekla, and herself. That might be the best way to handle it.

Stan's caterpillar eyebrows were wriggling.

"Dad?" she asked.

"Hmm?"

"If you feel okay, why do you look so funny?"

Shrugging, he patted her on one knee. "I'm thinking. Trying to get hold of something half-lost. A piece of something. Something just out of reach."

"About work?" she asked, tentatively. "Projected earnings? Golden parachutes? Greenmail?"

"No, something else. More important. Further back. Some kind of uproar . . ."

"Well . . ." Val began drawing out the "l"s. Maybe her father was thinking about the same thing she was. "Listen—what if we had dinner with Tekla one night?"

" 'Take heart, take heart, O Bulkington . . . Up from the spray of thy ocean-perishing . . .' "

As Stan spoke, Valerie turned her head, surprised to hear him reciting words that sounded like poetry when she didn't know he'd ever read a poem in his life. She was sure he hadn't heard her question, and was about to repeat it when he answered.

"It's not a good idea," he said. Then, before she could question him, he straightened up. "Say—wait a minute. Where's my birthday gift?"

"Back at DeDe's. It's a box of pecan turtles."

As Valerie was speaking, she looked across at Stan and realized she was observing the same tooth-grinding stranger whose face she'd seen at dinner. "Why are we on BART? You're not well. We need to go home."

"Pecan turtles," Stan asked, blinking with amused disbelief. "Is that really what you said? Pecan turtles?"

Val nodded. Then she and her father dissolved into jittery laughter. The pecan turtles had shells of milk chocolate, which Stan wasn't supposed to eat. That was where the evening's troubles had begun. At least, some of them.

# 7

*Tatiana, dressed in a monk's habit, fled through the drifts of snow. Her feet were bleeding and wrapped in rags. However, just when she thought she couldn't drag herself any farther, she saw the lights of the town and began to crawl toward . . .*

". . . a booth at the Elite Café," Valerie was telling Tekla. "Look for me there about six. On the right, toward the back."

"Maybe I have plans tonight," Tekla said, her voice crackling through the receiver and needling into Val's ear. "It's Saturday, and you haven't given me much notice. Maybe I've made other arrangements."

"Oh. Have you?"

"Yes, but not till later. So I'll be there, as long as you promise you'll tell me what all this cloak-and-dagger mystery stuff is that you've been hinting at. Is it about your new book?"

"No, I have done seventy-four pages, but that's not why I want to see you. It's something else. You'll be there, won't you?"

"Okay. Sure. Yes." Even without seeing Tekla's face, Val could picture her raising one eyebrow and shaking her head skeptically.

As soon as Valerie had finished with Tekla, she went to work on her parents. One Saturday night a month, they allowed her to make plans for them, so she didn't anticipate any difficulty.

Claire, however, rejected Val's suggestion.

"But why?" Val asked. "It has booths. And this is important, very important."

"The food at the Elite is too spicy for your father's stomach."

"Not all of it," Val answered, prepared to dig in. She didn't want to have to call Tekla back and give her a chance to back out. "Dad can order the roast chicken or pork chop. He can have moussaka."

"Well . . ."

As soon as Val had overcome Claire's protests, she shut herself in her room, attempting to compose herself for the ordeal ahead. To please her parents, she even put on a pair of silver earrings with blue stones they'd given her for her twelfth birthday.

Shortly after six, when the Meyersons had already ordered soup, wine, and a platter of crayfish, Tekla made her way across the black-and-white tile floor and eased herself into the booth next to Valerie.

"Good evening, all," she said.

If she was surprised to see Stan and Claire sitting there, she didn't show it. Stan and Claire, on the other hand, were somewhat less composed.

They avoided looking at each other. Nor did they turn their eyes toward Tekla. They, too, appeared to know that T.J. preferred to be observed from an oblique angle. But they did examine Valerie, wordlessly asking why she'd neglected to mention that Tekla Reis was going to be joining them.

Val was about to summon up enough energy to break the silence when the miniskirted hostess, whose name tag identified her as Annie, did it for her. "I thought you were a threesome," she said, resting one hip against the edge of their table and peering into the booth. "You know we don't seat you here when you're still incomplete."

Stan and Claire raised their eyes. Claire nodded. Stan shrugged.

The hostess splayed her fingers on the tabletop, as if she was waiting for a better explanation. Tekla leaned forward and patted her hand. "We're all incomplete. Each of us in one way or another is incomplete, or would it be too Chekhovian to say, 'We're in mourning for our lives.' So, we're sorry, Annie. You'll have to forgive us."

Annie, the expression on her face indicating she thought Tekla was dangerous or slightly mad or both, turned and fled.

Tekla took a crayfish from the platter and snapped it in half. While she was picking the meat out of its tail, Stan lifted up a crayfish and broke it in two.

"No," Valerie told her father. "You're not supposed to eat that."

"Be quiet," Claire whispered.

Stan put the tail in his mouth and began sucking on it noisily.

Tekla looked from one face to the other. She flicked the orange-colored shells onto Val's butter plate and wiped her hands on Val's napkin. "Mountain climbers," she declared, "as they are about to scale a particularly dicey piece of rock, say it's very *interesting*. And there's an ancient Chinese curse that says, 'May you live in interesting times.' "

She paused while the busboy placed silverware, a napkin, and a wineglass at her place. When he retreated, she poured herself some wine from the carafe in the middle of the table. Then, lifting her glass, she continued. "I'd like to modify that, Claire, and say to you and Stan, 'May you have interesting daughters. Or *an* interesting daughter.' And you do. She's interesting, very, very interesting."

After a moment she turned and began to examine Valerie. "Now I think it's time to tell us what's on your mind."

Val opened her mouth. She closed it again.

Claire jerked her hand sideways and sloshed wine into her salad. Ignoring this, she straightened her already straight shoulders. "No, don't."

"It's all right," Stan said. "It will be okay. Val, go on. Speak up. We're all grownups here."

Aware that her vocal cords were oddly constricted, Valerie began to speak. "I've figured it out," she said.

The three others sat there without responding.

"I know, Mom, why we don't look anything alike. You don't have to pretend that I have Aunt DeDe's chin anymore. And, T.J., I know why I look so much like you."

"What?" Claire asked.

Valerie twisted one blue-and-silver earring and smiled at her. "I love you, Mom. I still love you and always will. You've raised me, and you're my mom.

It's just that I know now that Tekla is my biological mother, that you asked her to do this after all those miscarriages when you thought you'd never—"

"What?" The word exploded like a firecracker from between Stan's teeth. "Why, that's the wildest, most preposterous—"

"I've seen the scar," Val said, forging ahead.

"Does the fourth wish to order?" Annie asked, twitching a menu down in front of Tekla.

Tekla pushed it aside. "More crayfish," she said, without glancing up. "And more wine."

"And then T.J. didn't want to give me up after I was born, and you all got into a fight. When I get to Main Library, I'm going to use the microfilm machine to check the newspapers to see—"

"Stop, Ducky, stop. Please stop," her father insisted. "You've got this wrong. There's not a shred of truth to this theory of yours. It simply isn't true. Val, this is all fantasy. Total fantasy. About as probable as *The Magic Butter Churn*."

"Besides," Claire said, "we've got pictures. Pictures of me pregnant. And take off that hat, will you, so we can see your eyes."

Valerie lifted the Borsalino and tipped it onto a hook at the side of the booth. "But you were always pregnant. Even Bennett said so when I asked him."

Stan took hold of two more crayfish and bit each one in half. "I can't believe we're sitting here listening to this rubbish. If you weren't taller than I am and if I believed in corporal punishment of any sort, I'd turn you over my knee and wallop you."

"But . . ."

Frowning, Val turned toward Tekla. She had rehearsed most of this dialogue while alone in her room, and so far no one had said anything she hadn't anticipated. She hadn't expected the three of them to stop protecting her and confess to a secret that had been buried for more than twelve years. All she wanted was for them to know that she knew.

"T.J.?" she asked. She was sure that Tekla would have something meaningful to say.

Although she'd half-expected to find Tekla's eyes brimming with tears, Tekla seemed detached from the emotion swirling around the table, as if she were only a lightning rod grounding the electricity generated by this storm. Instead of feeling safe or cherished, Val felt as if she'd been foolish enough to take shelter under the tallest tree in the meadow. Or she was the tallest tree in the meadow.

"Val," Tekla said slowly, "let's try some other conversational gambit. Molly Moore tells me you've been pestering her. By phone. By letter."

Val tried to stand up, but she couldn't. All she succeeded in doing was scraping the tops of her knees against the underside of the table. Defeated, she slumped back and clasped her arms across her chest. "Did you have to change the subject?"

Tekla nodded. "Yes, but I don't have to be sitting here eating crayfish. I don't even like crayfish."

"But—"

"Pipe down," Tekla told her. "And I *can* talk to you that way, because I'm *not* your mother, so I don't have to listen to any crap. Nor do I have to consult guides written by famous pediatricians or by Bruno Bettelheim, for God's sake. I don't have to protect your fragile psyche. So listen to me. Are you listening?"

"Yes."

Barely pausing for breath, Tekla continued. "Once upon a time, there was a delicious and unusual little girl. She grew and grew, until one day she was suddenly too big for her britches. A wicked witch—that's me, 'cause I'm the wicked witch, always was, always will be, typecasting, I guess—befriended her. And this witch fed her gingerbread instead of bread crumbs and lured her with promises of fame and riches. Inexplicably, she took pity on the child and spared her from being zapped, which had been the fate of all the other delicious little girls and boys who'd ever been foolish enough to get in her way. And the witch listened to the too-big little girl, talked to her, gave her certain liberties about her house." She paused. "Are you beginning to get my drift?"

"No," Val confessed.

This was not in Val's prerehearsed script. She was lost. Stan and Claire, on the other hand, looked less upset than they had a few minutes earlier.

Stan had pushed his minestrone soup aside and was, instead, dismembering crayfish. Claire had abandoned her salad and begun to use a cocktail fork to split crayfish and spear the tail meat. Streaks of red sauce radiated like a fox's whiskers from the corners of her mouth onto her cheeks.

"And so, Valerie," Tekla continued, arranging empty shells in a scaly tower on her plate, "if the too-big-for-her-britches big-little girl wants to continue to enjoy any privileges at all at the house of the wicked witch, and if her parents will permit her to come to the little house again—which they might not and which it would be well within their right not to permit—she'd better not bring up any of this again. Because if she does, I'll fire up my oven, zap her, and serve her for supper with catsup and mustard. And the only thing that will be left then will be"—pausing, Tekla gestured—"the shell. A shell to toss out in the garbage like many other shells."

Valerie swallowed, but she didn't speak.

Some of what Tekla Reis was saying was clear and other parts of it were not. But Val got the gist.

"Do you agree?" Tekla asked, speaking directly to her and not to either one of her parents.

"This feels like blackmail," Val mumbled.

"Exactly," Tekla told her. "You are catching on. There may be hope for you yet."

Valerie looked at her father, at her mother, and then back at Tekla. They were all waiting for her answer. "I agree."

Suddenly Val's head felt cold. The others were looking at her, too, making her uncomfortable. She reached up, grabbed for the Borsalino, and put it on, pulling it down over the curly hair that was so much like Tekla Reis's. Although she needed to go to the rest room, she was unsure how she'd manage to extricate herself from the booth.

Tekla reached out and touched her shoulder. "I'd like you to apologize to your folks for causing such a fuss."

"I'm sorry," Val said. She was, but she wasn't. There were still secrets swirling in the air above their heads, and she resented knowing that things were being kept from her.

"No matter what silly ideas you may have gotten into your head," Claire told her, "and they were silly ones, you are our daughter, our real daughter, and we love you."

Stan leaned forward. "I second what your mom just said. Emphatically. Now, relax and have something to eat, will you?"

With an obedient nod, Val began to slather butter on a piece of French bread. Then her father turned toward Tekla. "So, do you still have your country place at Glen Ellen? Your cottage in the redwoods?"

"Yes," Tekla answered, "though I don't get up there as much as I'd like."

"Well," Claire asked, clearing her throat in the new way Val had just begun to notice, "are you writing? What are you writing about now?"

"About life." Tekla's voice was as noncommittal as each of theirs. "That's what your interesting daughter says she is doing. And that's what I'm trying to do, too."

Then Tekla slid over and stood up. Val raised her eyes. Now Tekla—her friend T.J.—was a stranger, too. A thin, dark-haired stranger with graying streaks spilling down from the center part of her head and a mole on the left side of her chin. Lines arched from the corners of her nose to the edges of her mouth. Twisting around her neck was a thin scarf in a jolting shade of yellow.

"You don't have to leave," Claire told her. "We haven't had dessert. Their crème brûlée is particularly good."

"And I don't have to stay either. Staying would be pointless. We don't have anything to talk about. And besides, I don't think I can sit here any longer and watch your husband poisoning his gut with those disgusting orange cephalopods."

Tekla's words were washing over Valerie. She was hearing them and yet was too upset to really listen. Her eyes were stinging, but she blinked hard, determined not to cry.

Then Tekla was looking at her again. "I owe you an apology, too. But I had to be that way," she said. "I'm sorry, because a lot of this is my fault, and none of it's easy. Val, your folks may not want you to keep coming to see me, and if they don't, you'll have to understand. If it *is* okay with them, however, you know where I am. You can find me at the house. Or even up at Glen Ellen. You can come some weekend, if you'd like—meet some other writers."

Then, reaching out, she mashed Valerie's hat down over her eyes. By the time Val had shoved it back again, she could see only the end of a yellow scarf snaking out the front door into the dark.

# 8

*Suddenly, overcome with shyness, Saralinda drew back. She and Derek hadn't seen one another in a year, not since she'd gone in search of her past. Still, as they lingered under the willow trees, she shivered when he touched her fingertips and said . . .*

"I'm not going to hear some self-important writer read from his work! Besides, I disagree with what you're doing."

Listening to her father's voice, Valerie pressed herself flatter against the wall and hoped she wouldn't be discovered. She'd been drawn from her room when slamming doors alerted her to the fact that something was happening at their end of the house. Storm warnings had been in the air ever since the dinner at the Elite Café. It had been, Val felt, only a matter of time before the tornado hit them full force.

Val was trying to break herself of the habit of eavesdropping, but she felt justified by the circumstances. Her parents had denied Tekla was her mother, yet T.J. had said only that Val was never to speak about it again.

If Stan, Claire, and Tekla had nothing to hide, why would they have reacted so vehemently to Val's suggestion? There were, she was convinced, still secrets swirling about.

"But this is E. L. Doctorow. He's very famous," Claire insisted, using a too cheerful tone of voice. "He's the man who wrote *Ragtime* and *Loon Lake*."

"Have you ever read those books? Or anything else the man wrote? And don't you mistrust anyone who's afraid to use his first name?"

"Edgar," Valerie whispered to herself. "Like the boy in *World's Fair*."

One of her parents shoved a dresser drawer back in place, making the wall vibrate for a moment. Val drew back, weighing whether she should slink away to her room. Curiosity, however, won out over conscience.

"Well, I've seen the movie of *Ragtime*," Claire answered, her voice alarmingly close to where Val was standing. "You have, too."

The next exchange between Claire and Stan was unintelligible because of water splashing in their bathroom sink and the high-pitched jerk-and-whine of faucets being turned on and off.

As Val was about to retreat, the doorknob of the master bedroom rotated, emitting a series of clicking sounds. "It won't work," Stan said, flinging the door open.

Val froze.

"Because, Claire, there's just no way you can turn yourself into Tekla Reis."

"But that's not what I'm doing."

Stan, his hand on the edge of the door, was backing into the hallway. "Nothing I say seems to make any difference. This is not the way we should be handling this thing—fighting old battles, trying to be people we aren't. I disapprove and refuse to take any part in it. So, if you want to go to this lecture, if you think you have to compete with T.J., then do it alone. Deal me out."

As he closed the door and wheeled around, Valerie was cowering there, hoping her dark clothing would camouflage her and keep him from detecting her. When he paused and refocused his eyes, she began to prepare herself for the worst.

Stan stared at her. Then he blinked, as if he'd momentarily forgotten who she was. "Poison," he said, not bothering to reprimand her for spying. "That woman spreads poison wherever she goes. She ought to wear a skull and crossbones."

Valerie and Claire were in their seats waiting for E. L. Doctorow to be introduced. Bennett, who was using Stan's ticket, had not yet appeared.

"I'm really sorry Dad wasn't feeling well," Claire said, patting Val on the shoulder. "I'm sure this is going to be wonderful, and I know he's sad to be missing it."

Valerie nodded, but she didn't say anything. Claire was trying to be enthusiastic and to cover up for Stan, who'd never told either of them he wasn't feeling well.

"Maybe Doctorow will inspire you to ever greater heights with your writing. And maybe, sometime soon, you'll be willing to give your father and me a look at what you've been working away on. Mr. Litke says you've shown some of it to him and that it's wonderful."

Claire's voice wrapped itself around her and began

to squeeze her like a sheet of shrink-wrap plastic. Yes, she had shown some of her novel to Mr. Litke, but only after he'd confiscated the tablet she'd been working on during class. What she was writing was so personal, she felt embarrassed to have an English teacher poring over it.

Mr. Litke had never told Val it was wonderful. If he'd said that to Claire, it was because Claire had been checking up on her. Val sighed. Living with people who were trying to bury the truth was difficult enough without finding them prying into her secrets while she was trying to pry into theirs.

As encouraging yet empty words continued to burble from Claire's mouth, Valerie scanned Herbst Hall to see if Tekla was there. Tekla and her friends, Val knew, seldom missed a chance to hear another writer speak. She saw a lot of dark-haired people in denim, but none of them were familiar to her.

The lights in the theater were dimming and Claire was still speaking when someone snatched Valerie's hat from her head and dropped it in her lap. Then, before she knew what was going on, that person had kissed her cheek with a noisy, mocking smack. Sighing, she rubbed at her cheek with the heel of one hand. It was Bennett.

As she was trying to think of something scathing to say so he'd know she was offended by his behavior, the audience began to applaud as a medium-tall, weathered-looking man slouched toward the podium. His tweed jacket seemed too tight in the shoulders, and his hooded eyes shifted from side to side as if he was trying to figure out why he'd promised to be there.

After adjusting the microphone and stalling in every

other small way he could, he finally stared down at the lectern and began to speak. Val slumped in her seat examining him. His right eyebrow was rounded, but his left one arched quizzically. The eyebrows and his cropped beard combined to give his face a devilish appearance.

He was talking very fast, describing the time he'd spent in the library when he was growing up in the Bronx. Then he told about an interview he'd written for his high-school newspaper. He'd interviewed Karl, the longtime doorman at Carnegie Hall, a friend and confidant to dozens of famous musicians. When his teacher had wanted Karl photographed for the paper, Edgar Doctorow had had to admit there was no doorman named Karl. For a sake of a good story, he'd made him up. The audience laughed, but Valerie winced.

E. L. Doctorow didn't want to be in Herbst Hall any more than she'd wanted to read in assembly at Horton Middle School. Being a published writer, she'd assumed, was difficult because she was just twelve. But Mr. Doctorow was almost fifty years older, and he didn't seem to feel any differently. Neither did Tekla Reis.

When Mr. Doctorow talked about how every time he wrote a book, the book had a voice—characters who spoke to him and took him over—Valerie thought about her own writing. Saralinda and Tatiana seemed to be using their own voices to tell her what was happening to each of them. But sometimes their words didn't seem as convincing when she reread them as they had when she'd first written them down. Why was that, she wondered.

By the time Valerie stopped reviewing her own work

and tuned back in, she discovered that Mr. Doctorow was preparing to read from a book called *Billy Bathgate*, which he said was about a fictional fifteen-year-old hoodlum who lived in the Bronx in the thirties.

At first she had trouble listening to Mr. Doctorow because he read at an even faster pace than the one at which he'd been speaking. He seemed worried, as if he were wondering if he'd come on stage without remembering to check the zipper on his trousers. Then, suddenly, his words took over and she no longer noticed his discomfort. Billy Bathgate juggled and did amazing coin tricks. He bought cupcakes. He stood face to face with a famous gangster named Dutch Schultz, but most of all, he told his story with some of the richest and most dazzling words she'd ever heard.

Val forgot about her mother and father arguing, about Saralinda or Tekla or her cousin Bennett's sappy kiss, as she listened to the mesmerizing torrent of words. Then, much too soon, it was over. Mr. Doctorow reached for his water glass, and the lights went up in the hall. After taking several swallows of water, he smiled shyly at the audience. For the first time since he'd appeared, he didn't look hesitant or alarmed. He was asking if anyone had any questions, and he was looking right at Valerie.

As if she and he were alone, Val found herself leaning forward. She didn't remember raising her hand or hearing him call on her. But she was speaking aloud, addressing him. "How," she asked, "does someone like Billy—you said he was a street kid—know all those wonderful words? What is it that makes him able to do that? He talks in the *most* incredible way. Why? How come?"

The audience was very quiet. Mr. Doctorow was hunched over the microphone, repeating her question. Claire wasn't moving. Even Bennett didn't whisper anything snide. Still, Valerie felt that she'd made a fool of herself.

Turning sideways, aware that her face was flaming as blood rushed to her cheeks and ears, she sank back into her seat. If she'd had her way, a trapdoor would have opened beneath her and dropped her into the basement of the theater. She wanted to lower her eyes, but she couldn't do it. Mr. Doctorow was staring at her, and she was reluctantly returning his gaze.

"I worried," Mr. Doctorow said, at last, "about that for the longest time. In a very rough sense, Billy is a kind of Huck Finn. So why *is* he so eloquent? It's very peculiar. I couldn't figure it out myself. Writing, however, is full of happy accidents, and there is an answer to your question. But if I tell you that answer now, it will give away too much about the rest of the book. So, I'm afraid, you'll have to read it to find out. Is that all right? Do you understand?"

"Your question," Bennett said, swallowing a mouthful of pepperoni pizza, "was brilliant. And, at least for tonight, I take back every awful thing I've ever said to or about you."

Valerie picked a slice of green pepper from the wedge on the plate in front of her. She was pleased, for once, to have Bennett's approval. Claire, who was twirling the stem of her glass of red wine, obviously felt differently. Val suspected that her mother, being unliterary, hadn't understood what she'd asked. Now Claire was depressed because Stan had been right when he told her there was no way she could turn herself into Tekla Reis.

"The question of voice—who's speaking, whose point of view a book takes—" Bennett declared, in his best freshman-English voice, "is so complicated. I'm amazed you saw this."

"Mmm," Val answered. Bennett, she was deciding, meant what he said, but he was being patronizing. Or he was trying to impress her mother. Claire, however, didn't look impressed. She looked displeased. She wasn't eating pizza or drinking wine.

She seemed to be wishing she were somewhere else. Val felt the same way. If she'd had a choice, she'd be home in bed writing the rest of the episode about Saralinda's romantic reunion with Derek. The only problem was that Valerie's life didn't include any romances she could incorporate into her work.

Derek was fictional, even if he did look a little like Bennett. They both were tall, with wavy blond hair. They both flung their arms about as they spoke. As Val was considering this accidental similarity, she noticed that Bennett was doing something Derek would never do: using his forefinger to dislodge a piece of pepperoni from between two of his molars.

Although Bennett did have some disgusting habits, his life was full of the type of experiences she needed to know about. Now that he seemed less critical of her, perhaps he'd confide in her, revealing what went on between him and his various Kates. She wouldn't need any experiences if she could get him to talk about his.

When he caught sight of Valerie eyeing him, he extracted the finger, rubbed it under his chin, and grinned at her. "You're looking good, coz. And when you start wearing some makeup, you'll look even better." Then he turned to Claire. "Little girls do grow up," he said.

"Sometimes faster than we like," Claire answered, letting her eyes scan the restaurant.

Val decided to ignore her mother's reply and concentrate on winning Bennett to her side. "I'm working on a new novel," she told him, "called *The Changeling*. I'm about to talk to my editor about it. The only thing I can't figure out is if I need an agent."

Bennett was frowning, but Val didn't know if this was in reaction to her words—which even she had found smug and embarrassing—or Claire's. Now Claire, instead of paying attention to either of them, had begun to stare at something or someone in one corner of Spuntino's.

Val swiveled her head and, after a moment, realized that Tekla was over there, seated with Lenore and several other people. One of the women at the table looked like Fred, the would-be actress from Stanford who'd lawn-bowled with them. Tekla and her friends were involved in an animated discussion. Maybe, Val told herself, they were talking about the question she'd asked E. L. Doctorow. She wished she could be with them as they tried to figure out how a hoodlum could speak like Billy Bathgate.

Val glanced back at Claire. Things were not going well for her at home. These days, if Claire wasn't arguing with Stan, she was either trying to be more like Tekla or being exasperated with Val. And if this didn't change soon, Val might have to see if she could live with Tekla for a while.

With a sigh, Val turned toward Tekla again, hoping

she'd look up and see her. Maybe she'd come over to the table and say, as Bennett had, how perceptive she'd been.

"Valerie?" Claire's crisp tone punctured Val's reverie.

"Yes?"

"Don't even think of getting up and going over there."

"What?"

Claire cleared her throat. "I said, stay where you are. Do it for me, if for no other reason. Please . . ."

"What's wrong, Aunt Claire?"

"Nothing."

"Is it Uncle Stan? Is he worse again?"

"No," Claire told Bennett. "He's fine." Although her voice was low and even, the knuckles of her clenched hands looked like white marbles. "But this daughter of mine has her head filled with delusions—literary ones and ones about herself and the rest of us. Yet she's failing math, her adviser says, and getting C's in science."

Mr. Litke was not only her English teacher. He was her adviser. That's why Claire had been talking with him. He might even have called her. Val peered over her shoulder again, hoping Tekla would come to rescue her from this scene. Tekla, however, was shaking her head, engrossed in what her friends were discussing. She did not seem to be aware that Val was there.

Valerie looked sideways at Claire. "I think you're jealous of Tekla."

"Not really," her mother said, fumbling in her purse for her car keys. "Wary, perhaps. Also piqued, confused, sad, suspicious, perplexed, concerned—"

"But, Mom . . ."

"Aunt Claire . . ."

"You're twelve years old," Claire said. "Just twelve." Then she turned toward Bennett. "I mean, how does this all strike you? She's only twelve and already preoccupied by the idea of fame, unable to tell imaginary things from real ones. Adoptive mothers. Surrogate mothers. Writers. Other famous writers. My editor. My new novel. Do I need an agent? Tonight Val thinks she's a meteor, because she asked an important question. She didn't even know what was significant about it. Now she's sitting here acting pretentious, yet she can't even do her algebra assignments and hand them in on time."

Valerie kept waiting for her mother to raise her voice or start flinging soggy pizza slices around, but she didn't. Val was disappointed. If there was going to be a scene, she wanted it to be a big one, so T.J. would overhear them and take an interest in what was happening to her.

"This is a mess, and it's wearing me down."

Valerie wanted to jump to her feet and answer her mother, but she didn't do it. Partly because she understood why Claire was angry with her and partly because she was afraid Tekla Reis would refuse to look up and acknowledge she was there.

# 9

*With Derek's hands supporting her, Saralinda stood in the courtyard and watched the figure in the hooded monk's robe draw closer. Saralinda's knees were trembling and her hands were clammy as she scanned the shadowy face, looking for traces of . . .*

". . . lipstick and mascara? You're not planning to go to school that way?" Claire was blocking the doorway so Valerie couldn't get by.

"But I didn't use very much," Val said, hoisting her knapsack onto one shoulder. "Your face is so pink and white, you don't know how it is to look drab all the time."

"Go wash it off. Please. Besides, the kids at school will give you a tough time about it. If you feel drab, why don't you stop wearing that hat and put on something that isn't black for a change?"

Turning around and going to wash her face would be the simplest thing Valerie could do, but she and Claire weren't discussing lipstick or mascara. Claire was probably upset because she was wondering if Val still

87

thought Tekla was her mother. Well, she did, yet she didn't. One moment Val would be certain. Then doubts would circle her head like a cloud of whining mosquitoes.

These doubts were making Val suffer. In English class, Mr. Litke had told them that writers needed to suffer in order to produce great work. He'd said that when they were reading a story by Kafka about a man who woke up one morning and found he'd turned into a dung beetle. So far, Valerie had not felt herself developing any such tendencies, but her mother seemed to be growing antennae and a set of pincers.

"Stop holding on so tight," Val pleaded. "I love you. I'll always love you. Nothing's going to change."

Claire stepped aside, allowing Valerie to pass. "It already has." She sounded distant and distracted. "Maybe I should call my mother and tell her that I never before appreciated what I'd put her through. Or perhaps I should call my office and tell them that I've reconsidered and will head up the long-range planning task force."

Instead of answering, Val edged past her mother and let herself out by the kitchen door. As she bent into the wind and hurried off toward school, she wondered what she might have done differently. She hadn't screamed at Claire or said she hated her as other classmates of hers did when they got furious at their parents.

Valerie hadn't had much practice at this sort of confrontation. Usually, if one of her parents was out of sorts, the other one helped smooth things over. This morning, however, her father hadn't been anywhere in sight. Had he been cowering in the hallway, unwilling to support Claire when she was being unreasonable? Or had he, still angry at Claire from the night before, left for work this morning without waiting for her?

As Val was pondering these questions, a series of raucous squeals attracted her attention. Looking up, she saw Jo and several other students from Mr. Litke's homeroom huddled together on the school steps.

Ill at ease, Val paused and put one hand over her mouth. She was still wearing the lipstick and mascara, but she didn't think she was close enough for them to have noticed. Maybe they were hooting and howling about something else: Miss Priss's mustache, or that article in the morning paper about the woman who planned to hold her daughter's wedding a second time because the videotape hadn't come out. For a moment, Val stood there, remembering how she used to hang around and gossip with them.

Then, exercising strict self-control, she lowered her hand and slowly forced herself to approach them. "Hi," she said.

"Hi," Jo answered. "You look different. I wish my mother would let me wear makeup."

"Mmm . . ."

"Are you on the best-seller list yet?" one of the boys asked. "How's your new book coming?"

Val put a hand up to her mouth again. "I'm not sure."

"Is it juicy? Wild? Scary? Do you think it'll be made into a movie?"

These questions were alarming. Although Val had written over a hundred pages of her new book, she often felt as if she weren't really a writer. Nor did she feel like a middle-school student. Why had she approached her classmates this morning? She'd forgotten how to talk to them. Squeezing her eyes closed, she saw herself as an acrobat walking on a tightrope high above the sawdust floor. She opened her eyes. Her classmates, like all circus spectators, were staring at her, seeming to be unsure if they wanted her to reach safety or to fall.

Unable to deal with this situation, Valerie wheeled and turned away. "I forgot something," she mumbled, looking back over one shoulder. She was leaving. She'd get in a lot of trouble for cutting school again, but she was off balance there and needed to be someplace else.

While Valerie stood on the front steps pressing the bell, she tugged at a strand of ivy and watched its brown tentacles tear loose from the porch railing. Khan appeared, undulated his silvery body against her ankles, then disappeared. Val leaned on the button again.

"Answer it," she begged. "You must be there. It's me, and it's important."

When she pressed her ear against the door, she couldn't hear footsteps or any other sign of life. With increasing despair, she pounded the door with the heel of her hand.

At last, as she was about to give up, she heard a voice. "Who's there? What do you want?"

The voice was drifting up from somewhere below Valerie's feet. It was Lenore, whose apartment doorway was under Tekla's porch. Tekla, she said, was already gone for the weekend. She and some other writers had gone to T.J.'s house at Glen Ellen, because they were teaching at a poetry conference at Sonoma State.

"Are you going, too?" Val asked, leaning over the porch railing and trying to sound casual.

Lenore, dressed only in an oversized T-shirt, appeared to have been asleep when Val began pounding on Tekla's door. Stretching, she raked her fingers through her cropped taffy-toned hair. "Eventually," she said, stifling a yawn.

Valerie wasn't sure how to phrase what she wanted to ask, so she just loosened her tongue and let it do what it would. "Have you got room? Can I come along? Hitch a ride? I need to talk to T.J."

"I'll give you the number, and you can call her."

"No, it's more complicated than that. I have to do this in person. I've got the first hundred pages of my book, and I want her to look at them. I won't stay, if there isn't room, and I'll find my own way home. But I need to see her today."

Instead of arguing with Valerie, Lenore shrugged and beckoned. "Come down, while I get ready. It's an hour's drive, and I hate driving up alone. T.J. will be pissed with me. But so what? And, of course, all the way up we can talk about writing, about the process of writing. You'll like that, won't you?"

Valerie could hardly believe her good fortune. Lenore hadn't even asked why she wasn't in school, so she didn't have to manufacture lies.

She had her yellow tablets in her knapsack—the two completed ones, and the third on which she'd just begun writing about the reunion of Saralinda and her real mother. The tablets, although important, were not as significant as what she needed to ask Tekla.

While Lenore was getting dressed, Val flicked through the stack of *New Yorker* magazines she found on the kitchen table. In Val's experience, *The New Yorker*—except for the ads and the cartoons—was a boring magazine. The stories always ended before the end. Then when she tried to read the poetry, she usually got bogged down and found herself wondering why almost every poem seemed to have a tree in it.

She decided, while waiting for Lenore, that the tree, branch, or leaves in most *New Yorker* poems would be a good discussion topic for the ride up to Tekla's house in the country. It would help convince Lenore that she was mature enough to grapple with sophisticated literary issues. It might even make her warm up and begin to like Val.

But Valerie never had a chance to discuss *New Yorker* poetry because Lenore sang Broadway show tunes from Lombard Street in the city until they were turning off Big Stony Road into T.J.'s driveway. Except for "Memories" and "Don't Cry for Me, Argentina," they weren't songs Valerie knew, so she couldn't sing along. The only conversation they had during the drive involved whether *West Side Story* was a better musical than *Oklahoma!*—and since Valerie hadn't seen either one, all she could do was nod and say, "Hmm . . ."

By the time Valerie opened the car door and stepped out in front of a shingled cottage nestled under a grove of redwood trees, she began to have qualms about what she had done. It was after eleven. If someone from Horton had phoned her parents at the bank, they already knew she wasn't there but wouldn't have any idea of where she was. She needed to talk to each of them, but she couldn't do that before she spoke with Tekla.

Tekla, however, was not immediately available.

When Val and Lenore opened the front door, they found sleeping bags unrolled on the living room floor and breakfast dishes glazed with dried egg yolk on the kitchen table, but no sign of Tekla or her friends. In fact, the place looked as if it had been ransacked by a band of burglars.

Lenore, seemingly undiscouraged by this sight, dropped her own sleeping bag onto the floor, snagged a muffin from a basket on the table, and burst into the chorus of a song called "I Am What I Am." Then she turned and headed out the kitchen door toward the woods. Valerie, not knowing what else to do, trailed after her.

Still singing, Lenore tromped along a narrow trail through the trees. Valerie, her knapsack dangling from one shoulder, did the same. Although the sun was shining, under the redwoods only slanting ribbons of light filtered down to the forest floor, where the air was cool and sweet-smelling. The edges of the trail were fringed with pale lily-like flowers. If Val hadn't begun to feel anxious, she would have enjoyed their scent and beauty. Later, she hoped, she'd have time to appreciate Glen Ellen.

Beside the path was a shallow, white-water stream, and its splashing noises swallowed Lenore's voice. It also distracted Valerie from hearing the others until they nearly stumbled over them. Tekla was with another woman and two men. They were sprawled out at the edge of the water.

Flinging out one hand, Lenore stopped. The other she raised to her lips to gesture for silence. The scene before them seemed oddly familiar, Val thought, resembling a famous painting she'd seen in an art book.

There was a picnic cloth with fruit and wine. The men, instead of being dressed for hiking, were wearing black jackets and floppy bow ties that looked like the ones her mother wore to the bank. Tekla was wrapped in a bed sheet, and the other woman didn't have any clothes on at all.

Val squinted. She'd been wrong. The woman was wearing a flesh-colored leotard and flesh-colored tights. Lenore and Valerie stood at the edge of the copse, unobserved. The other four were talking quietly, but their voices were somehow magnified by the configuration of rocks and trees.

"But how could you have done it, T.J.?" one of the men asked. He was lying on his back with his head in the lap of the woman in the leotard.

"Curiosity. Obsession," Tekla said, trailing the edge of her bed-sheet dress in the water. "I was tempting fate. It was a stupid lapse. And, besides, he'd said she was so talented."

As Tekla was speaking, she glanced up and caught sight of Valerie and Lenore. "Hello there," she said.

Valerie edged forward. "Were you talking about me?"

Tekla shook her head. "No, someone else. A student of mine, but it might as well have been you."

"Am I?" Val's heart was pumping in her ears.

"Are you what?"

"Talented."

"I dunno, Sweet Pea. Maybe. Maybe not. Producing your kind of work at an early age is sometimes not real talent but just a trick done with mirrors."

"Are you the young writer T.J. told us about?" the reclining man asked. "You are. My God, you're so young. Oh, T, how come you let a vulture like Molly get hold of her?"

Tekla lifted the wet hem of her sheet, wrung it out, and began to scrub her face with it. She seemed uncharacteristically edgy and unwilling to meet Val's eyes. "M.M. found the story on my desk and said it was a naïve version of *Alice in Wonderland* and that she *had* to have it."

"That's awful," the woman in the leotard said. Then she turned toward Val. "If you can't produce, child, Molly's going to drop you like a hot potato."

Listening, Valerie felt her knees begin to buckle. To ward off a rush of dizziness, she knelt in a patch of ferns. She wanted to press her hands against her ears and shut out all their words, but she couldn't make herself do it. Nor could she manage to speak.

Lenore was looking down at her with a kittenish smirk on her face.

"Molly never takes on a book without having a follow-up in her back pocket," Tekla said quietly. "There's another piece of juvenilia. About a horse. M.M.'s decided it's a naïve *Moby-Dick* but with a horse instead of a whale."

"Oh, no," Valerie cried out, scrambling back to her feet. "Not *Wildest Horse in America*, not that dumb thing. I'm working on something new, and it's so much better."

"It will have to be," Lenore said, speaking directly into Val's ear. "Because you're not going to get by as a writer by being cute. You're going to have to produce and be judged—just like the rest of us."

Valerie had wrapped herself in the quilt she found on the bed in the room with the walls that were a mottled mossy green. She wasn't crying. In fact, she hadn't permitted herself to cry at all. She'd simply fled from the group by the stream. Then, once she'd reached the house, she'd lain on the bed, rubbing her fists into her eyes and trying to figure out what to do next. After a while someone opened the door, came into the room, and sat on the edge of the bed.

A hand tugged at one edge of the quilt and peeled it away from Val's face. It was Tekla's hand, and Tekla, her forehead furrowed, was examining Val's face.

"Where'd you get those black eyes?"

"Black eyes?" Valerie asked.

"Oh, never mind." Tekla released her hold on the quilt and edged away so she wasn't sitting quite so close to Val. When she spoke again, her voice was soft and oddly hesitant. "Are you okay? I'm sorry about all that—before."

"I'll live," Val answered, trying to sound composed and under control, which wasn't easy when she was lying there wrapped like an Egyptian mummy.

"We shouldn't have talked to you or about you that way. But you stole up on us while we were in the middle of a discussion. Besides, eavesdropping is a terrible habit. Don't do it. Sooner or later you'll always end up finding out something you'd rather not know."

"You sound like my dad." Valerie struggled to free her arms. Then, rolling onto her side, she propped herself up on one elbow. "Is my writing—like you said—some kind of trick instead of a real talent?"

"That's what Lenny thinks, but I'm not sure."

"I don't like her very much," Val said.

"Oh, she's all right," Tekla insisted. "Though I

haven't a clue why she brought you up here, because I'm working and have a conference to put on."

"I know, but I wanted to give you the first hundred pages of my novel. And, since things are kind of rocky at home, I was thinking I could live with you for a while."

"What?"

"It was a dumb idea."

Tekla extended one hand. Then she dropped it into her lap again. "Not dumb. Just not possible."

"But you understand me so well, T.J. You care about the same things I care about. We're alike."

"Maybe. But I'm still not your mother. You know that, don't you?"

"Yes . . ." Valerie whispered reluctantly.

"So why has it taken you so long to face up to the truth? No, forget it. Don't answer. I do understand. Sometimes unreality is easier to deal with than reality. Listen, and don't get upset—your dad called before. He's coming to get you."

Val closed her eyes. "How did he know I was here? How will he find this place?"

"He knows the way. Hey, are you okay?"

"Yes. Will you read my new book?"

"Sure. But if I don't like it, I'll have to tell you. Will you be able to handle that?"

"I don't know." As Valerie answered, she opened her eyes and began to inspect the blotchy paint on the wall. "It looks mossy," she said. "Like the moss on the trees near the house."

"It's supposed to. Glazing, the technique's called. Took eight coats and a ton of rags to get it that way, and you're the second person who ever noticed it's like the moss without being told. Val . . ." As Tekla spoke her name, she reached out and fingered a lock of Valerie's hair. "Val?"

"What?"

"Is your dad's stomach still bad, or is he feeling better?"

Valerie rolled away, threw off the quilt, and staggered to her feet. "Huh?"

"Your dad?"

"Oh. Dad. Yes. He's better, I think."

Crossing the room, Valerie peered at herself in the oval mirror over the bureau. In the mirror, she could see Tekla's dark head nodding. Her scalp began to prickle. Something was wrong. How *had* her father known where she was? And why did Tekla seem to be so concerned about how he was feeling?

Leaning closer to the glass, as if that would help answer these questions, Val realized that she did look as if she had two black eyes.

Then, a moment later, she began to giggle nervously. "It's the mascara," she said, addressing not Tekla but her reflection in the mirror.

# 10

*When Saralinda raised her eyes, she was gazing at a pair of eyes like her own—twin pools of blue, deep and murky. The hair, too, once the monk's hood was thrown back, was familiar with its halo of dark ringlets crackling about her shoulders.*
*"At last," a voice whispered. "At last, I've found..."*

". . . the prodigal daughter! You've led us on quite a chase. I don't know whether to be angry or relieved."

Valerie raised her head. At the same moment she took the yellow pad marked "III" and slid it back into her knapsack. "Daddy," she said.

Stan was leaning over the bed, peering down at her. "Your mother's fit to be tied. You're too old, you know, to be running away from home. When you were little, at least, and pulled this sort of stunt, you stopped when you got to the corner."

"I stopped," Val told him, "because I wasn't allowed to cross the street."

"Yes, things were simpler then. A rule was a rule. They were our rules, and it never occurred to you that you had any right to be making them. So, why are you doing this? Why?"

"Don't . . ." Tekla said. "Please."

Tekla was standing behind Stan, her fingers pinching the sleeve of his shirt. Then, as Val was watching, she dropped her hand and stepped back toward the doorway of the gray-green bedroom.

"The walls," Valerie informed her father, sitting up straighter and gesturing with one hand, "are painted to look like the moss on the redwood trees. T.J. said I was only the second person who ever noticed that without being told."

Stan nodded wanly. Valerie didn't know if he had pains in his stomach or if he was trying not to lose his temper. "They're glazed. I know. Now come on. Get up."

"Take it easy on her," Tekla said.

"Don't tell me how to deal with her," Stan answered, turning toward Tekla. "Claire and I are doing all right. We may not be experts on the care and feeding of adolescents, but your perceptions are even less valid."

"Why should that be?" Tekla's eyes were zigzagging along the random planks of the wooden floor. "I was a child, too. And I remember twelve."

"I didn't know you then," Stan mused. "And I certainly didn't know myself when I was that age. But I'm perceptive enough to see that this triumvirate is throwing everything out of kilter. This has got to stop. I have enough other things on my mind."

"What?" Tekla asked.

"What?" Valerie echoed.

She pushed the quilt aside and sat staring down at her crooked baby toes. She felt as if the words Tekla and her father were speaking were in some other language or in a code, which she was just beginning to crack. In another minute, if she listened carefully, she might begin to understand what was really going on.

"I'm not emotionally involved here," Tekla said, leaning against the doorway of the mossy room, "which may make my suggestions a lot more valid than yours."

"Not emotionally involved," Stan declared. "The hell you aren't!"

Valerie jumped to her feet and rushed forward, placing herself between Tekla and her father. She turned from one to the other. "What's going on? What are you talking about?"

Stan reacted to Valerie's words by lurching sideways as if he'd been stabbed. Next, moving slowly, he lowered himself into the chair near the door.

For a moment, no one said anything.

Then Stan straightened his shoulders. "Sorry. Gut pain. But it passed. And this, too, shall pass. Like everything else. It's just being here, T, in this place. Makes me into someone else. I'm sorry. I need to lighten up."

Tekla turned to Val. "Go wash your face." Her voice was impersonal and only vaguely friendly. "Or whatever. I think your dad should take you home. Now."

Without pausing to question Tekla, Val fled and locked herself into the bathroom. While she was there, taking a very long time, scrubbing the mascara from her face, she tried to make sense of what she'd just seen and heard, but she couldn't do it.

After she'd spent a long while washing, she began to be aware of voices drifting in under the door. They were coming from the living room, where Lenore and

Tekla's friends were talking and laughing in ordinary, everyday tones. How, Val wondered, after the tense scene in the bedroom, could she join them and take part in relaxed chatter?

Looking down, she realized that Tekla's washcloth was smudged with black. Taking hold of the bar of shriveled, brown-streaked soap, she tried to coax the telltale marks from the cloth. They were stubborn, however, and didn't want to rinse out.

Finally, unable to procrastinate any longer, Valerie emerged from the bathroom. The conversation she'd been overhearing was now animated enough to bounce off the walls and assault her ears. Lenore and Tekla's friends were lounging around the fireplace drinking root beer and eating popcorn.

"And then," Lenore said, "he picked up the book and demanded that he be given the role of Helena!"

"No way!"

"Come on."

"I love it."

"Is that true?"

"Absolutely. Said all of *A Midsummer Night's Dream* would make more sense if Helena was played by a man."

Stan—or a person who looked somewhat like him—was leaning against the mantel with an odd, keyed-up expression on his face.

More laughter rose in waves and pushed against Valerie.

"T.J.? Is that true?"

Tekla, who was busy wiping down the tile counter between the kitchen and the main room, looked up. "True."

"And such a pretty girl he was—even if he did refuse to shave his mustache."

What were they talking about? What was so funny? Val felt as if she'd stumbled upon a children's birthday party to which she hadn't been invited. Suddenly, to make matters even more confusing, Val's father—the preoccupied banker with the recurring stomach pains—began to hoot boyishly.

"And then T.J. showed him how to walk in a dress, taking little steps, shaking his hair away from his face."

By now Stan had stepped away from the fireplace and was standing with his arms held stiffly away from his sides. " 'I am your spaniel; and . . . the more you beat me, I will fawn on you.' "

"Oh, it's true, and you remember," the woman in the flesh-colored bodysuit said. "Let's do a scene. There's a Shakespeare here, and we'll do the other roles. That would be more fun than outlining poetry seminars."

Valerie was perplexed. "A play?" she asked, stepping forward and interrupting the flow of their laughter. "You were in a play, Daddy, doing the part of a woman?"

Stan hiccuped self-consciously. "Oh, no, Ducky. Not me. I've never been on a stage in my life."

"Then what?" Val asked, aware that her questions had only increased the level of merriment around her.

What was wrong, Val kept asking herself, that things kept happening which made so little sense? At Tekla's, Stan seemed like a different person from the one who lived in her house with her.

"But I don't understand," she said, aware of a tiny V-shaped scar on her father's forehead she'd never noticed before. "Weren't you talking about a Shakespeare play? About being dressed as a woman?"

As she was speaking, Stan's expression changed, shifting from a smile to a grimace of pain.

"It wasn't a play," Tekla told her, moving sideways and placing one hand on her back. "Just a play-reading group we used to belong to years ago—in another life—before you were born. Back then, we had time and psychic energy for that kind of thing. But those days are long gone. Over. So get your knapsack, and your dad can take you home to your mother, who's going to be even more worried if you don't get home soon."

"Can you imagine my dad in a play-reading group?" Valerie asked Bennett as she filled the big pot up with water.

"No. But then, I can't imagine my dad blowing on a clarinet or my mom figure-skating."

Val, glad to be with her cousin instead of her parents, added salt, clapped on the lid, and lit the front burner.

Somehow, when Stan brought her home, she'd managed to bear up under Claire's anger and anxiety. After sputtering out an uncountable number of "How-could-you's," Claire had withdrawn into a cold silence. Now she and Stan were at a reception to meet the new head of marketing for the bank. Although no one was willing to say so, Bennett was baby-sitting, as he used to do when she was younger. Her parents were afraid to leave her alone, fearing she'd run away to Tekla Reis's again. Bennett was more of a guard than anything. Her keeper. Was he being paid by the hour? Maybe, instead, her parents had promised him tickets to a rock concert, as they used to do when he spent an evening with her.

"Or your mom figure-skating," Bennett continued, beginning to arrange carrot and celery sticks end to end in an elaborate maze.

Valerie fished for the lettuce leaves that were floating in the sink. She laid them in scalloped ruffles on a bed of white paper towels.

"My father used to collect butterflies and play goalie on his high-school soccer team, too. But even those things are more believable than play-reading. Why, *Cats* is the only play he's seen in the last five years, and I know he never *reads* them."

"The secret life of Stanley Meyerson," Bennett intoned. "Is that what you mean?"

Reaching out, Val destroyed one corner of Bennett's maze by picking up several carrot sticks. She began to add them to the lettuce ruffles, making what appeared to be a headless woman with orange arms and legs.

"A few weeks ago, on his birthday, he quoted poetry to me. Then, today, it was Shakespeare."

Shrugging, Bennett dropped into a kitchen chair. "Do you think something suspicious is going on?"

"I'm not sure."

"Well, if you do, why don't you listen in when he's on the phone?"

Annoyed by Bennett's suggestion, Valerie rearranged some of the lettuce and added a carrot top. Now she had a pregnant woman with orange extremities, an orange face, and lacy green hair.

"For a while," she said, eyeing the silly figure, "I even thought Tekla Reis was my mother."

Bennett spewed morsels of celery in her direction. Then, shaking his head, he forced himself to swallow. "Not a chance, Miss Zany Imagination. Your mother is Claire Meyerson. You know Claire—the curvy little blonde who used to figure-skate with my mom. The Sims Girls. The Gliding, Sliding Sims Sisters. And she sewed their costumes, too. Put the sequins on by hand."

"Sequins? My mom? Nope. She can hardly sew a button on—much less sequins. Maybe you heard it wrong. Still, they do have too many secrets, and no one tells me anything I want to know. I'm sure there's some kind of mystery here. But no matter how much I figure out on my own, there's so much that no one talks about."

"About your father?"

Nodding, Valerie slid into the kitchen chair opposite Bennett. "Yes." She leaned forward and propped her chin on her hands. Maybe she was beginning to get somewhere. Perhaps Bennett would confide in her and reveal all the family secrets. "Exactly. I mean, if he used to read poetry and do play-reading and doesn't do either anymore, there must be other things to find out, too."

The salted water was beginning to boil. Puffs of steam were seeping out from under the lid, but she didn't get up to add the pasta. "Like what happened," she began, "with my father and Claire and Tekla Reis? Back when they were play-reading and doing whatever they used to do when they were still friends?"

Bennett frowned.

"What?" she repeated.

"Beats me," he replied. "I thought you wanted to know about the surgery."

"Surgery?"

Clouds of wet steam were warming Valerie's face and beginning to fog up the kitchen windows. The lid of the aluminum pot made a monotonous clattering sound as it rose and fell with each jet of steam.

"Your father's."

Valerie jumped to her feet, reached for a towel, and grabbed for the lid. Even with a towel, the heat from the lid seared her fingers until she let go, watching it roll down the kitchen floor like a steaming silver hubcap. It wobbled, spun, then thunked to a stop next to the kitchen door.

"Valerie! Listen. Pay attention. Your father, Stanley, the one who drove all the way to Glen Ellen today to retrieve his runaway child. He's scheduled to have a colostomy next week. I thought *that's* what you meant when you said no one ever told you anything."

"Surgery? Dad? My dad? You see? I was right," she wailed. "They don't tell me anything. I didn't know. When was this decided?"

"Well, they've been doing tests, but the decision wasn't made until this morning. If you hadn't flown the coop, cousin, and caused so much trouble, I'm sure they would have remembered to tell you."

"Surgery? That's ridiculous. There's nothing wrong with him. This is just a banker's disease, like Mom's bad feet, only the pain's in the stomach. No one needs to cut into him for that."

"Valerie! Val!"

Staring into the pot of roiling bubbles, Valerie ignored

Bennett. With a lunge, she took hold of the package of fettuccine and raised it in the air above her head. Then tears began to well up in her eyes. "But this can't happen," she said, lowering her arms. "There's already too much going on. My old book. My new book. Tekla Reis. Molly Moore won't talk to me. Nothing's going right. Everything's wrong, and everyone's lying about everything. And now my father's really sick, too."

"Val," Bennett said, prying the fettuccine from her fingers. "Stop overreacting. Your dad's not going to die. He just has a bleeding colon that they can't seem to control with medication. Therefore—a colostomy."

Valerie was sobbing by now. She couldn't seem to stop. Bennett, dropping his usual superciliousness, stepped forward and draped his arms about her shoulders, squeezing her, yet at the same time holding himself away. "Don't. Please. Everything's going to be fine."

Leaning her head against his nubby oatmeal-colored sweater, she continued to cry. "Maybe not. Maybe never again. Things used to be so simple, and now they're so complicated . . ."

Even as she was saying this, however, she was aware that it felt good to have someone hugging and comforting her. Even Bennett. He had, after all, begun to seem more and more human. "Take it easy," he said in a tone that was wary yet soothing. "Everything's going to be okay."

"Is it?" she asked, pulling away and wiping her nose on the edge of one black cuff.

Bennett nodded. "Sure. They just cut out a section of the colon, rejoin it, and route it to the outside, where there's a bag to collect waste. Then that's it. No more bleeding or pain. Your dad's very stoic. He'll be happy to trade in that pain for a rubber bag. And then, if all goes well and the rest of the colon heals, they may eventually be able to reconnect him."

Valerie was listening, yet she wasn't really listening. She didn't wish to hear the details of her father's surgery. They would make her worry too much. But there were other things she did want to hear. Things Bennett could tell her if he would. About her parents. About the strange sensation she had when she'd heard her father quoting poetry or the delicate way Tekla had pinched at her father's shirt sleeve instead of reaching out and grabbing hold of his elbow.

# 11

*The girl felt as if she was peering at them through layers of greenish-gray moss. She tried to flick it aside, but it still blurred the picture of her father and the poet. The two of them were connected as the poet twitched the striped cotton of her father's sleeve between her fingers; yet—at the same time—they were separated by an invisible pane of glass. She sighed. It was . . .*

". . . time to leave for the hospital."

Valerie looked up from her yellow pad.

"Sorry to interrupt you, Ducky," her father said. "But we're on our way."

"I don't understand why you didn't tell me sooner. Why you kept it from me."

Stan sank down next to her and wrapped one arm around the bedpost. "Easy . . . easy. We've covered that ground already. You were preoccupied. We didn't want to get worked up in advance, because this operation's not cancer or anything like that. And it's going to change my life. Fifteen years of pain and worry are about to be over."

Val examined her father. There were hairs in his ear, folds of skin on his neck she'd never noticed before.

"I want to come with you, be there to keep Mom company."

"Not this morning." Val swiveled her head. Claire was standing in the doorway with a small duffel dangling from one hand. "I'll be just fine. Besides, you've missed enough school already."

"But, Mom—"

"Stop. Don't. We've had too many tantrums lately. So today, for a change, please do as we say."

" 'You are my sunshine, my only sunshine,' " Stan sang, apropos of nothing.

"Come on, Mom, you're being unreasonable. Daddy's having surgery. They're going to cut him open."

When Claire cleared her throat, Val noticed an odd, involuntary twitch ripple across her right cheek. "DeDe will be with me. First there's the check-in. Then additional laboratory tests. Then, near noon, the operation. But that will take several hours—when you add in the time for anesthesia and such. Then they'll keep him in the recovery room, monitoring bleeding and vital signs, so none of us will see him until late afternoon."

Claire was being as clinical as a soap-opera doctor describing a medical procedure about to be performed on some faceless minor character. Her suit was pressed, her shoes were polished, and her bow was tied this morning with greater precision than ever. If Val took a ruler, she was sure she'd find each loop measured the same.

"Val? Are you listening? Put away your novel, and gather up your school stuff. We all need to get going."

"It's not my novel."

"It looks like it," Claire said.

"Well, it isn't. Tekla has my novel."

"Okay, whatever . . ."

Stan stood up. Scratching his head, he examined his wife and then his daughter. He seemed to be trying to decide how he could deal with the fire smoldering between them. "If it's not the novel, what are you writing?" There was a false heartiness to his tone. "Have you finished the new novel?"

"Not yet."

"Maybe, after the surgery, when I'm convalescing, you'll show it to me. To your mom, too."

"Maybe," Valerie mumbled.

"Don't be like that, please. How about a hug and a kiss? One for your mom, too." Stan reached for her hand, but Val drew it away and used it to press the yellow tablet against her chest.

"Oh, let her be," Claire said, stepping forward and taking hold of Stan's arm. "She's so overwrought these days that it's hard for her to be concerned about anyone except herself. She thinks she's the hub of the universe. And we did it, Stan, by permitting Tekla Reis to stalk back into our lives and stir her up. If she doesn't snap out of it soon, she'll fail eighth grade."

"Claire?" Her father's voice had a pleading tone to it.

Claire nodded. "Okay. Come on, hon. We're supposed to be at the hospital now."

"Val?" Stan asked, flapping one hand in her direction.

With a sigh, Valerie placed her tablet face down on her comforter and got to her feet. Her mother was right.

She had been behaving miserably, and she felt ashamed of herself. But, still, she was angry at their attitudes. Resisting an urge to straddle the bedpost, to fasten her fingers around Stan's wrist like handcuffs so he couldn't escape and expose himself to the dangers of surgery, she leaned against him and kissed him on the cheek.

Next she stepped sideways and brushed her lips against Claire's ear. Then, before either of her parents could say another word, Val picked up her hat and headed out of the house.

When she reached Geary, a bus was approaching. It was going in the wrong direction, but on a whim she stepped forward and boarded it. One more day of playing hooky could hardly matter. Besides, she needed time by herself—time to do some thinking.

Maybe, she thought, as her father was being wheeled into surgery, she'd be crossing Market Street and walking toward the Seventh Street Bus Terminal. Then, by the time the surgeon was using his scalpel to remove her father's colon, she'd be standing in line to purchase a ticket. Later, just about the time her father was being rolled from the operating room to the recovery room, she'd be boarding a Greyhound to New York, so she could settle some things with Molly Moore. It might take her three or four days to get there, but she had all the time in the world.

Once she arrived, she'd go see Molly, ask if her writing ability was a talent or a trick. Later, she'd send a postcard of the Empire State Building to Stan and Claire, and one of the stone lions at the Public Library to Tekla Reis. Then—

Suddenly someone plodding along on a side street

caught Val's eye. Lurching to her feet, she jerked at the cord. She had a better idea. It would make more sense than planning a pretend trip to New York. Val was going to have a real adventure, something unusual to write about. Again she tugged at the cord, but the bus continued to careen ahead. When the driver reached a corner where he was willing to stop, she shoved at the door and hurried down the back steps to the sidewalk.

Without pausing to consider where she was, she ran back up O'Farrell and turned onto Hyde. Ahead of her, she caught sight of the person she'd spotted from the window of the bus. It was Fred, the actress from Stanford. Today she had a stocking cap pulled down over her hair and a stained orange blanket wrapped around her shoulders. Val had recognized her because she was pulling her wagon.

"Fred," Val called, racing along after the clattering wagon. One wheel was loose and it wobbled. Fred had taken Lenore's advice and roughed the wagon up so it wouldn't give her away by looking so new. "Fred, wait up! Wait."

Fred didn't pause or turn as Val closed the distance between them. As her feet pounded the pavement, she remembered something. "Fred" was just an alias. The actress had told them her real name. It was something like Sara or Moira or Farrah. No—wait. She did remember the woman's name.

As she reached out to touch the blanket, she was calling that name. "Laura, Laura. It's me—Valerie!" She had only an instant's warning that the shoulder she was touching was too broad to be Laura's before it angled sideways and wedged her into a shadowed, paper-littered doorway.

"What do you want?" a croaking voice asked. "It wasn't Fred's. It was Sig's. And I didn't take it. Besides, it was my knife."

Panting, Valerie struggled to make her eyes focus. She wasn't looking into the face of Laura the acting student but at the leathery, unshaven face of a wild-eyed man. He had a tooth missing in front. He smelled of mildew and rotting cheese.

The man's arm and elbow were gouging into her. He'd said something about a knife. She didn't see one, but that only frightened her more. She was going to vomit or wet herself. Or both. Her mouth was dry. When she opened it, no sound came out. Her eyes were dry, too. She couldn't even cry. While her father was undergoing surgery with a sterilized instrument, she was about to have her throat cut with a rusty knife.

Her hat had slipped sideways and was partially obscuring her eyes. She'd begun to shake. Cars were passing by. She could hear them, but everything seemed distant, flattened, as if it were only a movie screen's version of a street scene with sound and light but no depth.

"Some things you just have to do." The man tapped the front of her sweater with stubby, calloused fingers. "I'm not going to let that drunken witch take her, put a spell on her. Understand?"

Valerie tried to nod or offer some kind of answer, but she seemed to be paralyzed. She'd been held in this position for an hour now. Or perhaps for a day. Time seemed to have stopped.

"Understand?" the man demanded.

"Yes . . ." Val managed to whisper.

She was still shaking, but she was still breathing, too. She was alive, and if she could only get her brain to work, she might figure out how to stay that way.

"Social workers get younger and younger," the man muttered, looking over his shoulder as if there were someone else there he might be addressing. "This skinny one only looks about *twelve*."

As Valerie was edging away from the man, she heard a small, whimpering noise, and the rags in the wagon shifted to one side.

He wheeled around, dropped to his knees, and bent over. Now Valerie was free. All she had to do was twist sideways and dart out of the doorway. But she stayed where she was.

She couldn't leave. There in the wobbly wagon, wrapped in bundles of rags, this desperate man had a stolen baby. She had to take action, do something brave, save that child and return her to her rightful mother. A baby needed to be with its mother.

"Wait," she pleaded. "Don't." What was the man doing? Was he dropping to his knees so he could plunge his knife into the helpless baby? But the man was peeling back the rags gently one by one, rooting through them to take hold of the child.

Valerie could see only the top of the baby's dark head, but she chose that moment to spring from the doorway and grab hold of the handle of the wagon. The man flailed his hands in her direction. "She's mine. Mine," he cried. "I traded my knife to Sig. Fair and square."

As Valerie was about to streak off, towing the wagon

behind her, she heard a yelp. Then, as she stood there, a nose emerged, and two round eyes. The baby in the wagon had a tail, too, which it was wagging.

All the wild-eyed man was protecting was a puppy, some kind of bony, thin-haired chihuahua. Valerie dropped the wagon handle and began to run.

"Thank you," the man called from behind her. "It fits, too. Very classy, and I can use it. It was a trade. We traded. Right? Thank Fred for me."

The ragged man was crazed, but at least he wasn't pursuing her. Valerie ran and kept on running north with her feet slapping against the pavement. Even when she'd escaped from the Tenderloin District, she continued heading north and farther north, uphill, then downhill again, until, at last, she came to the door of Tekla's Russian Hill house.

Too agitated to ring the bell, Val began to pound against the slab of redwood. After a long moment, the door opened.

"What are you doing here?" Tekla asked. "Do you know how early it is? People aren't even out of bed at this hour." Despite her words, Tekla was out of bed. She was wearing jeans and a black-and-yellow-checked shirt. Either she'd already been up and showered or she'd never gone to bed. "All right. Come in. What's going on? Is something wrong? It is."

Valerie stumbled inside. She'd run for blocks and blocks with the kind of adrenaline rush she knew only from swimming. But she was here now where she could collapse and be comforted.

But Tekla wasn't reaching for Valerie or soothing her. Instead, Tekla was shaking her. When the shaking didn't provide the kind of result Tekla was looking for, she raised one hand and cuffed Val on the side of her face. "What's happened? Is it your father? It is your father, isn't it?"

"What?"

"Your *father?*"

Confused, Valerie nodded. As she was nodding, Tekla leaned forward and folded her arms around her. Bony fingers pressed against Val's back. Val inhaled and smelled the unmistakable odor of stale cigarettes.

"Tell me. Quick, tell me."

"This morning," Valerie said, struggling for breath. "At eleven. It's scheduled for eleven."

"What?" Tekla dropped her arms and held Val in front of her. "You mean they haven't operated yet? Nothing's wrong, yet you come here and scare me half out of my wits?"

Reeling backwards, Val leaned against the dark wood paneling in the entrance hall. She looked at her watch. It wasn't nine o'clock, yet every one of the people she really cared for had already yelled at her this morning. She'd been threatened by some crazed man. And, to make matters worse, her father was having his stomach cut open and they wouldn't let her come to the hospital. It was too much. She began to cry.

"Stop it," Tekla said. "I never know what to do when someone cries."

Valerie went right on crying. Soon her cries turned into racking sobs.

"When people are very needy, it makes me feel claustrophobic. So stop, please. Now—before I lose my cool and push you out the door onto your skinny little ass."

"I thought you cared about me."

"I do."

"Not really," Val replied, experiencing a sudden flash of insight. "It's not *me* but my father you care about. You're a terrible person, and I hate you."

There was a long silence, broken at last by the sound of Tekla's voice. "Well, at least we agree."

While her comment was still echoing in the dark hallway, Tekla stalked away from the door and returned with something yellowish and oblong, which she handed to Valerie.

"Here. You have a way with words, but your choice of subject matter stinks. This is garbage. If it were mine, I wouldn't even use it to line the litter box. I'd bury it."

Valerie caught herself in the middle of a sob. She hiccuped and looked up. It was her manuscript that Tekla had given her, Val's legal tablets covered from end to end with the saga of Saralinda and her long-lost mother.

"But I worked so hard. I—"

"Student writing is always puerile. Also florid and banal. Especially the sex scenes. Sex scenes? Have you ever *done* any of those things?"

"No."

Tekla rolled her eyes. "Well, Lenny's rule of thumb says: if you haven't done it, don't write about it. And now—since you know how I feel and won't, I'm sure, ever want to have anything else to do with me—you might as well leave."

Valerie sniffed and swallowed. She narrowed her eyes. She wasn't going to cry anymore. How could she ever have imagined Tekla was her mother? She couldn't be. There was something cold and dark and damaged about her. Valerie had had enough. If Tekla Reis didn't

119

like her or her work, if Tekla thought she had no talent, she'd never trouble her again. And Tekla might be right about Val's lack of ability. But—still—there was one last thing she wanted to know.

As she was about to speak, something behind Tekla moved. Val angled her head sideways and saw Lenore curled up on the living room couch with Khan in her lap. She had a smug grin on her face, because she'd enjoyed every minute of this scene. If Lenore and Tekla were the kind of people writers were, Valerie wasn't certain she wanted to become one. And she surely wasn't one yet. *The Magic Butter Churn* made her an author, but it had not made her a writer.

"Looking into your closet," Lenore said, chuckling, "must be like looking into the closet of a vampire. And where's the black hat? I'd begun to think you had glued it to your head."

Val reached up distractedly. "Gone. I guess. Lost."

Then, straightening her shoulders, she shifted her gaze so she was staring at Tekla while she voiced the question it had taken her so long to formulate. "What is it," she asked, "between you and my father?"

Tekla shook her head, but she didn't answer.

"You don't have anything to say?"

"No."

Valerie frowned. She nodded. Then she turned her back on Tekla Reis and walked out of her house.

# 12

*Saralinda was leaning against her mother's shoulder, holding her hand as she told her about the wild-eyed man who had threatened her with a rusty knife. "I've never felt so alone," she whispered. "So endangered. But, at the same time, it seemed as if some unpredictable stranger, wearing my body, had brought me there and was forcing me to...*

". . . wait. But not much longer. Just till the nurses finish changing the dressing."

Valerie looked up. Using her mouth, she recapped her pen. "What?" she asked, as she clipped it onto the front of the yellow tablet.

"I said, you can go into your dad's room in a few minutes. Your mother's there, and he's beginning to wake up. Everything's fine. He came through this like a champ."

The doctor who was addressing her had talked to her before, right after the surgery. He was a surgical resident. She'd forgotten his name, but not his face. His skin was yellowish and his nose curved slightly to the left. He had a limp and tired eyes. As Valerie stared at him, she suddenly felt that this was someone who could understand what she'd gone through, what she was—even now—going through.

He gestured toward her tablet. "What are you writing?" A lock of hair had fallen down over his forehead. "It looks like quite an undertaking. I used to write short stories, but yours looks more like a book."

Val nodded. Then, biting down on her bottom lip, she shook her head. Diamond. His name was Dr. Diamond. "I thought it was. But now I'm not so sure. A writer I know just told me that it's garbage."

Dr. Diamond tugged at his stethoscope. "Well, what does he know?"

"She knows," Val sighed, rising to her feet. "She says some writing is just a trick done with mirrors." Now she and Dr. Diamond were standing face to face in the greenish glare of the hospital corridor. She wanted to tell him about *The Magic Butter Churn*, about Tekla Reis, too. "Listen . . ."

"Yes?"

"If I can't see my dad for another five minutes, would you like to have a Coke with me? I'll pay." A cup of coffee would have been a more sophisticated suggestion, but Valerie didn't drink coffee.

Dr. Diamond shook his head. "Not possible," he said, his face looking even yellower than it had before. "I have to change and scrub for another procedure."

Valerie lowered her eyes. The surgical greens he was wearing had dried blood on them. Her father's blood, most probably. A wave of guilt washed over her. "I didn't mean it. I don't know what I was saying, because I want to see my dad as soon as I possibly can."

"Then you're in luck," Dr. Diamond said. "Because the nurses are leaving, and you can go in."
Quickly Val turned away.
"Wait," Dr. Diamond said.
"What?"
"You forgot your tablet."
"Oh . . . thanks."
"Maybe we can have that Coke at another time?"
"I don't know," she told him, feeling an embarrassed flush singeing the tips of her ears.

As she was hurrying down the corridor toward her father's room, she knew she'd never be able to talk to Dr. Diamond again. What had come over her? While her father was lying in a hospital bed suffering, she'd been flirting with a doctor almost old enough to be her father.

When she saw Stan, she felt even worse. He was tubed and bagged and ringed with stainless-steel poles. Monitors clicked and beeped as they assessed his internal condition. His breathing was hoarse and ragged. His eyes were closed and his left cheek kept twitching.

Valerie shuddered.

"What took you so long?" Claire asked, from her seat in the high-backed turquoise vinyl chair by the bed. "I thought Dr. Ruby was going to send you right in."

"He said I had to wait until the nurses were finished."

Peering through the dimness, Valerie examined her mother. Claire's voice was reedy. Her fine blond hair had a damp, greasy look to it, and her legs were so short that her feet didn't quite touch the floor. She looked like a little old girl who needed someone to put an arm around her shoulders. Valerie felt as if she should make the gesture, but she didn't.

Stan was groaning.

Valerie rushed to his side. "Do something," she said.

Claire shook her head. "It's normal, they say, part of coming out of the anesthesia. He can hear you, and he'll answer you, if you talk to him, but he's still kind of out of it."

"I am not," Stan replied in a voice that sounded as if it were coming from the bottom of a deep well. He opened his eyes. They were glazed. His eyes and face both had a gray cast. Valerie was reminded of the way dead fish looked, displayed on a bed of ice at the supermarket. All her father needed to complete the image was sprigs of plastic parsley.

"It's . . . why, it's Jane Eyre," he mumbled, squinting at Val. "How are you, Jane?"

Valerie blinked. She knew who Jane Eyre was, of course; she'd read Charlotte Brontë's book, like everyone else in Mr. Litke's eighth-grade class. But she couldn't imagine why her father would address her that way. He never had before.

"So, how are you, Jane?" Stan repeated, jerking at a piece of plastic tubing that was taped to his left hand.

"Don't do that," Claire warned, looking up from the magazine in her lap.

Stan closed his eyes. "Bossy nurses here," he hissed. Then, in a singsong voice, he continued. "But, Jane, tell me, don't you know there's a string, attached somewhere under my ribs, that connects to a corresponding one tied to your little frame?"

"He's not making sense," Valerie told her mother.

"He thinks he is." As Claire spoke, she began to flip

through the magazine, ripping out scented perfume ads and flinging them on the floor. Their flowery Great-Aunt Ida smell tickled Val's nose. She sneezed.

"Bless you," her father said. "I love those dark curls of yours. The dark lady of the sonnets. Three twenty-thirds. Wasn't that what you wrote? 'Take heart, take heart, O Bulkington . . . my cup runneth over.' "

Valerie leaned across the bed and touched her father on his right shoulder. She was anxious to change the subject. This conversation felt eerie and dangerous. Claire was pretending to examine her magazine and to take this babbling in stride, but she looked panicky. Valerie remembered how she'd felt when the man in the Tenderloin had shoved her into the deserted doorway and wondered why her mother looked as if she felt someone was threatening her in a similar way.

Val turned back to Stan. "Daddy, how do you feel? Does it hurt?"

"Does what hurt, Jane? The string tied between us?"

Val glanced at her mother again, but Claire refused to look up. "No, not the string—your *colon*, Daddy—I mean, where they took it out?"

Stan rolled his head from side to side on the pillow. His eyes opened, but he was staring at the ceiling instead of at Val. "No, you're mistaken. They didn't take my colon—only my wisdom teeth—and you promised you would stay with me. But you didn't. You were out listening to Robert Frost."

"Mom . . ." Valerie pleaded.

"What?"

"He thinks he had his wisdom teeth out."

"I know."

"I did," Stan insisted.

"You did," Claire agreed, reaching out and patting his arm. "Hey . . . shhh. Take it easy, honey. Relax. You're fine. I'm here. Now calm down."

"When?" Valerie asked, beginning to feel she had some inkling of what was going on. "When did he have his wisdom teeth out?"

"A long time ago. Before I knew him."

Valerie looked down. Her father's eyes were focused now and staring up at her. "What's wrong?" he asked.

"You're fine," Val told him.

"Yes, I am. But you look awful. What is it?"

"You didn't know me." Val was ashamed of the whiny tone in which she'd spoken. "You thought I was someone called Jane."

Her father took a deep breath. He winced, as if in pain. "There's only one Jane. Besides, I know you. You're my daughter, you're . . . Ducky. Isn't that who you are?"

Before Val could reply, someone knocked at the door and pushed it open. It was Aunt DeDe, and Bennett was with her.

"Bennett," Claire pleaded, in a voice that seemed not quite under control. "Take her. Do something with her. Stan's supposed to stay quiet, but he's getting agitated. Val can come back around dinnertime, when he's slept off all the anesthesia. You did say you had tickets to something at the Exploratorium, didn't you?"

"I was going to bring Kate," Bennett told Valerie as he was driving her to the Exploratorium. "It's her birthday, and that's what she wanted. But now she's not speaking to me."

"I thought her name was Keaton." Val propped her feet against the dashboard and leaned back.

Bennett shook his head. "No, you're mixed up. Keaton was the one before—the redhead. Kate's the short one with black hair and bangs."

"Whatever," Val replied, shrugging.

She didn't want to crawl through the Tactile Dome at the Exploratorium with Bennett. The Tactile Dome was where she and her classmates had wanted to go for their fifth-grade birthday parties. It was a maze of unlit passages through which one wriggled blindly, touching its varying textures and the available extremities of the person just ahead of you. A fifth-grade trip through the dome had always been an occasion for much squealing and self-conscious giggling. Three years later, however, it held little interest for her.

Although Valerie was able to imagine why Bennett might have wanted to grope through it with one of his Kates, she could see no reason for two cousins to do so. Especially when her father was lying semicomatose in a bed at Northpoint Hospital. She was even less enthusiastic when she realized that their companions in the Tactile Dome were going to be a troop of ten-year-old Boy Scouts.

"I've had a terrible day," she told Bennett as they stood outside the entrance panels while several of the boys pushed past them, chortling and making farting noises. "Can't we just pretend we used these tickets?"

"No," Bennett said, tugging at her arm. "Come along. This will loosen you up. You'll feel better. Be better company for your dad and not quite so much of a pain in the ass for Claire."

Only a moment later, Val found herself following the ridged soles of Bennett's socks through a passage paneled with Astroturf and remnants from rubber tires. The air seemed thick and stale. The boys, ahead of them and behind, kept shrieking. Val inhaled, but she didn't seem to be able to get enough oxygen into her lungs. The crawl spaces seemed smaller than the last time she'd been in the dome, the turns narrower. Some of the footing was precarious. She scraped a knee. She bumped her head. Then, because the tunnel seemed to end, she stopped and struggled to catch her breath. She couldn't. She was gagging and gasping.

"Val, what's wrong? Where are you?"

"Here." Her voice was a choked whisper.

"Get moving."

"I can't."

Making disgusted clicking sounds with his tongue, he edged backwards. "C'mon," he urged. "People don't just stop in here. There's no room to pass, and all those kids are behind us."

"I've got to get out," she said, clawing at his ankles. "I can't breathe."

"Valerie!"

"Please," she pleaded. "Oh, please."

"Val!"

"My dad's been cut open, a homeless person threatened me, I lost the Borsalino, Tekla said my writing is trash—especially the sex scenes—then I made a fool of myself with some doctor, and then my father didn't know me. He called me Jane Eyre."

"Easy. Easy. Your dad didn't really think you were Jane Eyre."

"No, he thought I was someone else."

"Who?"

Bennett's ankles were hairy, but she had no intention of letting go. "Someone . . ."

Bennett reached back and squeezed her hand. "Stick with me. We're almost at the Red Room. When we get there, you can rest, and you'll feel more like yourself."

Three or four turns later, Valerie let go of Bennett's ankles so he could help lift her up into the Red Room, which was the padded, pillowed conversation pit in the middle of the dome. The ceiling was low, so people had to lie down, and it was lit by a dim red darkroom-type bulb, but it did have some light and enough air. Val wasn't sure she'd make it through to the other end, but for the moment she was out of danger.

Bennett propped pillows under her head and draped one hand protectively over her shoulder. "See. It's better, huh? Now breathe slowly—in and out. Yes. Better?"

"Yes."

Several boys came climbing up and tumbling through the Red Room, snickering and nudging one another as they caught sight of Val and Bennett on the padded shelf.

"Wooooeee."

"Smoochy-smoochy."

"Oh, speak to me, darling."

"Bug off," Bennett told them, tightening his grip on Val's shoulder, "before I have to kick you in your canteens or in some other sensitive spot."

Impressed by the fierceness of his tone, the boys scrambled down the ladder and left.

"So . . ." Bennett said, speaking in a low, concerned voice. "Was there really a man with a knife and did Tekla Reis really say your writing was awful?"

"Yes."

"And the resident. Dr. Pearl? Yeah, Pearl. We met him out in the hall. Why would you waste your time talking to such a humorless geek?"

"Mom said his name was Ruby, and I thought it was Diamond."

"I don't think so. Actually, if you ask me, I'd say he looks more like a zircon."

Valerie laughed. She was beginning to feel more like herself. She stretched. She yawned. Then she began to realize something. Bennett's breath felt warm against her hair. Suddenly uncomfortable, she rolled away from him. He dropped his hand from her shoulder and began punching one of the pillows.

More Scouts appeared on their hands and knees, bringing with them the musty, sweaty smell of corduroy, gym socks, and locker rooms. Now they were belching and barking like dogs. Bennett, propping himself up, glared at them until they vanished into the labyrinth of unlit passages.

Then he turned back to Valerie. "But it's not any of that that's really bothering you, is it? Not even your dad's surgery. It's the other thing. Your folks—your folks and Tekla Reis." Bennett's voice was low. It had none of its usual sarcastic edge. He was, for once, taking her seriously.

"Yes," she told him.

"You said you don't still think she's your mother."

"I don't," Val answered.

"She might be someone else's mother, though. She was pregnant once. My mom told me so."

Valerie inhaled. She exhaled. "When?"

"A year before you were born."

Val tried to picture Tekla pregnant. She couldn't do it. She rubbed her forehead.

Bennett frowned. "You all right?"

"Yes. Yes, I'm fine. But what happened to the baby?"

"Mom didn't know."

"Are you sure?"

"All I'm sure of is that she has no intention of telling me any more about it. Or about what did happen, if anything, between Tekla and your folks."

Val pushed herself up so quickly, she grazed her head on the ceiling. "Ouch." She rubbed at it and leaned back so her head was resting against the wall. Bennett rolled over so he was slumping next to her. "So something *did* happen."

"Magic eight ball says yes. And, Val, listen, I've got another hunch, too."

"Hmm?"

"About Jane. Who Jane is."

Valerie licked her lips. "I already know."

"T.J. Reis. Tekla Jane. It must have been your hair and the bad lighting. He must have been remembering another time and another place."

"Mmm . . ." Valerie smiled at Bennett. She wriggled her toes. Never before had Bennett seemed so human. All day she'd felt so alone, but she didn't now. She was lucky, she realized almost thirteen years too late, to have a cousin who understood her.

Raising one eyebrow, Bennett examined her. "You

look good in burgundy. You should wear it more often."

Valerie giggled. "But I'm wearing black. It's just the light in here."

"It turns your hair red, too."

Val leaned closer to Bennett, so close she could see the edges of his contact lenses. By the time the Boy Scouts reappeared, she was about to try kissing him.

But she didn't. Abruptly, pulling back, she watched the boys, who had formed a centipede and were crawling past in an ominous, silent manner.

Bennett wiped his mouth on the sleeve of his shirt. "Tell me," he said, "you weren't thinking what I think you were thinking."

"I was," Val said, resisting the urge to run her tongue over her teeth and spit as she did when she brushed her teeth. "But then I came to my senses."

"Whew!"

"I would like to learn a few things, but not, I guess, with you."

"Actually, Val, you're kind of cute; however, kissing cousins are—"

"I know, I know—besides, I'm not your type, and my name's not Kate!"

Grinning, Bennett motioned toward the exit tunnel. "C'mon. Let's get out of here. You go first this time, and I'll stay right behind you."

"Right behind me?"

"Yes."

"Well, okay. But watch where you put your hands. I wouldn't want to have to kick you in your canteen."

Then, embarrassed by her boldness, Val turned away and, with Bennett following, crawled out of the Red

Room. Near the end of the route, where the passage opened up, she and Bennett both scrambled to their feet, but she was careful to avoid coming into physical contact with him.

"Okay?" Bennett asked.

"Yes. Fine. There's air here, too. I feel good—good enough to go back to the hospital now. Am I allowed?"

Bennett nodded. "You're allowed."

"But what am I going to do?"

"About gaining more sexual experience?"

Valerie punched Bennett on the arm. "No, dummy, about finding out about my family."

Bennett held the curtain aside, so Valerie could exit ahead of him. "Maybe you should forget about the whole thing."

"But I can't. You know that."

"Well, I guess, you're going to wait until your dad gets stronger. Then you're going to dig in and keep questioning him, your mom, and Tekla Reis until one of them tells you what you want to know."

# 13

*Saralinda and Derek were alone in the alcove lit only by the flames of the torch. His hand was resting on her shoulder, and she was aware of the warmth of his breath against the side of her face. Her mother, she knew, would not approve. But, still, he was gazing at her, asking . . .*

"May I pass?"

Valerie raised her head out of the water and pinched her nostrils. A man with dark curls and oversized, blue-tinted swim goggles was speaking to her. His skin was sallow, and his nose angled slightly to the left. He was wearing black neoprene gloves.

"Aren't you Dr. Ruby?" she asked.

"I am a doctor," he said, treading water next to her. "But my name is Perle. Marvin Perle. P-e-r-l-e. Do I know you?"

Val stared at his gloves, trying to figure out why someone would wear gloves in a swimming pool. "My father—Stanley Meyerson—is in the hospital. You helped with his surgery."

Marvin Perle nodded. "Oh, I remember you. I just

didn't recognize you without your clothes on. I mean—well—in a swimsuit instead of—well, whatever. Yes, I've got it—you're the writer. Right."

"Right," she echoed, disturbed to realize that someone so interesting-looking could have a name like Marvin.

"Well—listen—can I tell you something?"

"Sure. Anything."

"Okay—I don't mean to offend you, you know, but you're too slow for this lane."

Then, without waiting for her answer, he pushed off and launched into a butterfly stroke that made the entire surface of the pool rock with its water-slapping rhythm.

"Jerk," Val murmured, suddenly aware that her cousin Bennett wasn't alone in his ability to be alternately charming and despicable.

Dr. Marvin Perle hadn't even reassured her by saying that her father was getting along well. But he was. Everyone else said so. If there were no setbacks, he'd be released from the hospital at the end of the week.

Valerie had come swimming in order to work off the tension whirring inside her. The swimming was satisfying, but—after a six-week hiatus—she was out of condition, which was why Marvin Perle had complained she was too slow for the FAST lane.

Discouraged, she finished her mile and went to shower and dress. Then, without bothering to dry her hair, she headed for school. School had become a place where she marked time, barely conscious of the words prickling the air around her. There, too uncomfortable to make an effort with her classmates, she was completely alone. She'd begun to feel as if she were enclosed in a hard plastic bubble like the ones doctors used for sick children who were allergic to the world and would die if they emerged from the transparent cocoon.

This day began in a way that had become familiar. As she sat in a seat by the window in Mr. Litke's English class, she found herself writing the scene between Saralinda and Derek that she'd been composing as she swam laps at the pool.

Derek's lips were about to touch Saralinda's. Remembering, Val could feel herself shivering. Someone was calling her. It was Derek. He was chiding her. But he was addressing her by the wrong name. Instead of Saralinda, he was saying, "Valerie!"

Valerie raised her head.

It was Mr. Litke. His lips were still moving, but she could no longer make out what he was saying. Her hearing was impaired, because her classmates were murmuring, creating lapping waves of white noise.

She leaned forward. Mt. Litke appeared to be asking what she was writing on the yellow tablet. He was also suggesting that she come to the front of the room and read it aloud. This was not, she realized—aware that the plastic bubble was cracking, falling to the floor in jagged shards—a privilege being offered to an accomplished writer but a punishment being meted out for inattention in class.

Horrified, she sat where she was, watching motes of chalk dust spiral through a beam of sunlight. She couldn't possibly read aloud to her classmates and let them hear how Saralinda and Derek kissed by torchlight in the alcove of the castle.

"Since," Mr. Litke said, his voice beginning to project

clearly enough for Val to hear every word, "you find your own work more absorbing than *David Copperfield*, you ought to read some of it for us. We want to know if you've got a better first line than 'I am born.' "

Val could feel herself flushing with embarrassment and horror. Her writing was changing. In the ten days since Tekla had told her that her work was garbage, she'd begun to write differently, trying to include personal experiences, instead of writing about things she didn't understand. But what she was producing continued to be a disappointing mishmash of eggshells, orange peels, and coffee grounds. She was tempted to stand up and throw it in the wastebasket or out the window. She couldn't, however, because she found she was having difficulty seeing as well as hearing.

Maybe the bubble was fogging up. No, it wasn't the bubble. That had split and splintered at her feet. She was having trouble seeing because tears were filming her eyes. It was the second or third time in a week that she'd cried. Clutching the yellow tablet to her chest, she struggled to her feet.

Before she could move, however, someone took her by the elbow. Not Mr. Litke, who was still standing in front of the blackboard. It was Jo Samuels. Jo was offering Val a Kleenex, and she was telling Mr. Litke and the others that Valerie needed to be excused, because—according to what Val's aunt DeDe had told Jo's mother—Val's father had been through a serious operation and was still in the hospital.

As Val used the Kleenex to wipe her eyes and blow her nose, Jo kept talking and talking. She was saying Stan Meyerson would be in the hospital until Friday. That Val was under a lot of stress. That it would be cruel to make her read her personal work aloud if she didn't wish to. Mr. Litke, his head leaning to one side, was listening. Valerie took a deep breath, then another. Her teacher nodded. She was going to be spared. She wouldn't have to read aloud from her yellow pad. Not now or any other time, she told herself, vowing to take some kind of definitive action.

Now Mr. Litke was motioning for Jo to take her seat. He wasn't looking at Val anymore. He was, instead, asking the class to open their books to chapter 12 of *David Copperfield*. Val turned to Jo, who was sinking back into her chair at the other end of the aisle.

"Thank you," Val mouthed silently.

Tentatively, Jo smiled.

Valerie, trying to smile back, felt awkward and wondered if she should will herself back into the middle of the hard plastic bubble. No, probably not. The bubble's sharp fragments lay at her feet. Jo had defended Val for only one reason—because she cared. Val owed her a real thank-you and an apology, too.

As soon as school was over, Valerie offered them both. Then, after promising to call Jo later, she headed for the hospital, where she had other pressing matters to attend to. Because her father was doing so well, she decided it was time to ask him the questions whose answers she needed to know.

From outside the room, she heard a murmur of voices and knew Claire was with him. She was pleased. Now the three of them could talk. This was the moment for which she'd been waiting. She should have knocked. She knew that, but for some reason, she sidled in, allowing herself to stand unnoticed in the shadowed passageway by the door.

Stan's hands were up in the air. A string was stretched between them. It was an ordinary piece of white string, tied in a circle, that had been woven between his fingers into Jacob's ladder. A second pair of hands was reaching up and, in the dimness, tugging at the center of the string, easing it off Stan's fingers and onto her own.

"Cat's cradle," a voice said. "Now it's cat's cradle. I don't know how I remember these things, but I do. A little like riding a bicycle, I suppose."

It wasn't Claire speaking. It was Tekla Reis, and her father was making a strangly chuckling noise as he looked at T.J.'s hands. Tekla's chair was pulled up near the bed, but her face was turned away from the door, so Val couldn't see its expression. She could, however, see Stan. The chuckles settled deeper into his chest. They stopped. The expression on his face turned serious. He raised one hand and watched its shadow arch across the wall. Tekla shook the cat's cradle from her fingers. Then she lifted an arm, rotating her elbow until the shadow of her thin, elongated hand intersected with the shadow of her father's larger one.

Now Stan's face was angled toward the wall, and Val couldn't see its expression. She wasn't sure she wanted to. A lump was swelling up in the back of her throat. She tried to swallow, but she couldn't. Nor could she move in or out of her father's room. A series of vivid yet disconnected images spun through her head. The piercing sound of a violin concerto she'd heard once, the intense yellow of ginkgo leaves in the fall, the way she'd felt when a strange baby had laughed aloud at her in the elevator at Union Square Garage.

As Val tried to decide why these images were insinuating themselves into her consciousness, Tekla dropped her hand to her lap. Then, as she twisted the string around her index finger, she and Stan began to discuss a Gary Larson cartoon from the morning *Chronicle* and whether Claire should agree to head up the long-range planning task force at the bank.

When they started to debate whether San Francisco was spending too much money to keep the horse patrols in Golden Gate Park, Valerie was suddenly aware that Claire was standing behind her in the doorway of Stan's room. How long had she been there? Val had been so absorbed by the scene before her that she hadn't noticed, yet now, when she turned her head, she saw that Claire's eyes were opened wide, and her pupils were oddly dilated.

Still, before Val could move or speak, Claire did both. Her hand encircled Val's upper arm. "Stan, you must say something to this girl of ours. She's been eavesdropping again. I hope you two weren't discussing anything inappropriate for the ears of a twelve-year-old."

"Only horse patrols and how to do cat's cradle with a piece of string," Tekla told Claire, as she rose slowly to her feet. "I brought Stan the new Brodsky book, and then I was just hanging out, waiting for you to return, so I could say hello before I left."

"Valerie, this spying stuff has got to stop," Stan said, gasping with discomfort as he propped himself up straighter in the bed.

Valerie stood looking from one face to the other. Everything appeared to be so normal, so ordinary. Maybe it was. Maybe even the way the two shadow hands had met on the wall had been an accident. Or perhaps she'd imagined it. As she stood here in her father's room, nothing seemed unusual except for the intensity with which her mother's fingers were gripping her arm. Claire seemed, as she often did these days, to be seething with charges of electrical current.

Val shifted her weight from one foot to the other. Tekla was saying goodbye. Tekla was leaving. Claire used her free hand to blow Stan a kiss, telling him something about Valerie and fresh air. Then, only a moment or two later, Valerie—with her mother's hand steering her—was heading down the corridor away from Stan's room.

"What happened? What's happening?" Val asked.

"Keep walking," Claire said.

"Why?"

"Because I said so. Because you look green. As if you're coming down with the flu or something. I'm taking you out for a few minutes. We'll walk. The exercise will do us both good."

"But I swam this morning. I did a mile."

"Well, you can still use some air."

Valerie adjusted her long stride to her mother's shorter one as they advanced toward the elevator. When it arrived, they stepped in and rode to the first floor. Then, side by side, they crossed the lobby and out the door to the street.

When they were heading north on Cherry Street, Claire finally released Val's arm. "Whatever you saw—or thought you saw—you were wrong," she said.

"What is it?" Val urged. "What is going on?"

"Nothing," Claire said, in a voice that tried to seem casual but didn't manage to do so. "They're old friends. They knew each other before your dad ever met me."

Val tugged at the neck of her sweatshirt. "What are you saying?" she asked, not looking at Claire.

"It's complicated, and I'm not sure how to explain. It's not that I'm jealous. It's something else. More like being left out, yet not quite that either. You don't understand. Can't understand. You're too young."

"I don't think so."

After a long, brooding silence, Claire spoke again. "Your dad and I met through T.J.'s cousin. In our twenties, we were all friends and did a lot of things together. Then your dad fell in love with me. He married me."

"But something happened," Val said. "What is it that you won't tell me?"

They were approaching a medical building with slatted benches out in front next to an array of mailboxes. Claire stopped and dropped down onto the nearest bench. "Do you still think Tekla's your mother?"

"No. But Bennett did say that she was pregnant once."

"She was."

"When?"

"A year or so before you were born."

"And . . . ?"

Claire shrugged, but she didn't answer.

Val seated herself very close to her mother. "What happened?"

"Nothing. Everything. I'd had so many miscarriages by then, and it was an awful time. It seemed so unfair that Tekla, who didn't want a baby and hated children,

142

had gotten pregnant accidentally when I, who wanted a child, couldn't manage to have one. If it hadn't been such a stupid idea, I would have even taken T.J.'s baby."

"What?"

"You heard me."

"Why?" Val asked, aware that Claire, unnerved, was trying to blink back an uncharacteristic leakage of tears.

"I was desperate. I thought I'd be a good parent, and Tekla would be a rotten one."

A sharp pain was angling across Val's chest. She was having trouble breathing. "Did you ever ask?"

"No."

"Why not?"

"Because it would have been an unrealistic thing to do. But I was angry and envious."

A tear seeped over the inner edge of Claire's left eye and dribbled down the crosshatched skin next to her nose.

Val reached out and brushed it away with the tip of one finger. Then she put her hand on top of Claire's. "So you argued?"

Claire's hand was stiff, lifeless. She seemed to be having trouble breathing. "Not really. I was simply too obsessive and too crazed to be around her. Her pregnancy seemed a personal affront to me."

"What happened to the baby?"

"I'm not sure. An abortion, maybe. In any case, T.J. went away. Then I got pregnant with you. A wonderful yet terrifying time—until you were born, at midnight on a Tuesday. By the time Tekla came back, our lives had changed."

Claire's fourth finger, Val saw, was stained with minute spots of something that looked like blood but was probably red ink.

"Mom?" Val asked, putting a glob of saliva on her index finger and trying, unsuccessfully, to rub off the stain. What her mother was saying made sense, yet it didn't. Some crucial fact was being omitted.

"What?"

"Are you all right?"

"No."

"Can I help?"

"No. Not really. But don't worry. I'm going to be fine. I am fine."

"Then would you mind if I asked just one more question?"

Claire cleared her throat and the twitch reappeared in her cheek. She shook her head. "Please don't. I have my limits, and I've reached them. You—you and your dad both—think I'm cheerful. Perhaps. But I spent long enough being sad. And I don't like to be that way if I don't have to. Still, I am human. Too human. So, if there's anything else you must find out, ask your dad—or ask T.J."

Valerie lifted Claire's hand. She turned it over and sat examining the lifeline etched into her palm. There was something Val wanted to do. But it could wait. Right now she needed to stay with her mother.

# 14

*Saralinda sat on the iron bench stroking her mother Tatiana's hand, trying to make sense of the events whirling about them. "You're human. But I'm human, too," Tatiana was whispering. "Too human." Saralinda shook her head. She knew that Tatiana was wrong. Neither one of them was human. They were both stupid, phony, boring, trashy, unconvincing characters. They and the whole novel in which they appeared belonged . . .*

". . . in the garbage," Valerie mused, pushing her tablet away and taking hold of the telephone.

She reached Bennett, who—after some persuasion—agreed to come pick her up. If she planned to take action, this would be the last night it was possible. Tomorrow Stan was being released from the hospital. Then her comings and goings would, once again, be more closely monitored.

"Won't you tell me what this is about?" Bennett asked as they were heading toward the Golden Gate Bridge.

Val shook her head and cradled her knapsack against her chest. "Later. Maybe later. But not now. Besides, you promised you wouldn't ask questions."

"Well, I'm only human," Bennett insisted.

Val sighed. "Yes, I know, and so am I, and so are Mom and Dad, but that's the problem. At least part of it. But—never mind—you promised."

Valerie was addressing the back of Bennett's head. She was in the rear seat because she and Bennett were not alone. His new girlfriend, Wendy, was with them. She was a tall blonde whose hair had been cropped into some semblance of a man's crew cut. She should have looked unfeminine, but she had delicate features and was wearing a soft shell-pink sweatshirt covered with twinkling rhinestone stars.

Wendy made Valerie feel ugly and wish she'd done something to improve her appearance. Even tying back her hair with a colored ribbon might have helped. Well, she'd attend to details like that another time. Now she had something else to take care of.

It wouldn't be very much longer either, because Bennett was turning into the parking lot. A few minutes later, Val, Wendy, and Bennett were leaning into the wind as they followed the pedestrian walkway toward the center of the bridge. Valerie had wanted the other two to stay in the car, but Bennett had pointed out that it was night and dark and that he'd be irresponsible if he allowed Val to go alone.

When they reached the center of the bridge and were swaying there, dwarfed by the arching orange towers, Val bent down and began to unzip her knapsack.

"Oh, now I get it," Bennett said, as he bent over and caught sight of its contents. "We have to stand in the dark and freeze our tails off while my cousin—that fatuous, famous author—writes yet another chapter in her great American novel. Let's hear it for Valerie. Author! Author!"

"Ben, that's not nice," Wendy said.

Valerie took hold of her yellow legal tablets. "No, it's okay. I'm not sure what 'fatuous' means, but he's probably right. And, still, he's wrong, too." She stood up and leaned against the railing, looking out toward Alcatraz and the shimmering lights of the city. "You see, I'm not here to write in this novel. I'm here to drown it."

Bennett began to laugh. "Drown it? You're going to murder your novel by hurling it from the deck of the Golden Gate Bridge?"

Wendy frowned. "Stop," she urged.

Valerie was touched to see that Wendy was sensitive to her feelings, but she was also aware that Bennett was going to do and say whatever he wanted.

"So," he continued, "you're going to take something you've been working on for months and toss it into the Bay?"

"Yes," Val said. "One page at a time."

"But that would be littering. The highway patrol is going to stop and arrest us for malicious littering."

"Then I'll just fling it over."

"Great. It'll land on the deck of some Norwegian freighter and all the sailors will read it and come looking for you. 'For a good time: call Val.' "

"Stop!" she pleaded.

Ignoring her, Bennett flung out his arms and stepped sideways as if he were a basketball player assigned to guard her. "And besides, drowning your novel isn't even original. I read a book once—by McMurtry or

147

McGuane or one of those Mc writers—where the main character drowns his novel in the Rio Grande."

Valerie tugged at her knapsack, lifting it up. Then she jammed her yellow tablets back inside. She looked around. Her eyes scanned the western horizon. "C'mon, then," she sighed. "I've got another idea."

As Valerie and Bennett and Wendy heaped driftwood onto a crackling beach fire they'd built, Bennett shook his head. "Never boring," he muttered as he added more chunks of wood to the blaze. "Val has many faults, but being boring is not one of them."

Valerie was only half listening. She was sitting cross-legged, tearing pages off the tablets and crumpling them into tight balls.

"Hey—not yet. You have to wait for the coals," Bennett said. "Besides, maybe you'll change your mind. Maybe you don't want to immolate your novel on a ceremonial funeral pyre."

"But I do," Val told him. "It's making me crazy, and until I get rid of it, I can't do anything else."

While Valerie was speaking, she began to feed the pages of her novel into the crackling flames. The pages hissed, flared, and collapsed into accordion-shaped ashes. As she continued to set them afire, something strange began to happen to her. Her heart seemed to slide out of its usual place and migrate to a spot beneath her left arm, where it raced and caused odd, stabbing sensations in her armpit.

"Are you sure about this?" Wendy asked. "Maybe you should save it. And you're shivering terribly. Don't you want my sweatshirt?"

Val shook her head and kept adding pages to the fire.

Wendy pulled off the pink sweatshirt and wrapped it around Val's shoulders. "Keep it. It's yours. The sleeves are too short on me. Besides, you'll look good in pink." When Val glanced down, she paid little attention to the color of the sweatshirt. What did interest her was that each rhinestone star had become a tiny, hot, glowing point of fire.

"Okay. Enough," Bennett said, kneeling down next to Wendy. "Let's douse this thing and go."

The fiery stars were mesmerizing Valerie. "Not until I'm done," she protested, aware of a high-pitched, careening tone to her voice. "It's already dead. But I'm not going until it's all burned up. I don't want to read it again. And I don't want anyone else reading it either."

"Val?" Bennett asked.

"What?"

"Does this have something to do with your mom and Tekla Reis and Stan?"

Val looked up. "Something."

"What have you found out?"

Valerie shook her head. "I'm not sure. I'm still working things out, and that's why—after I finish burning this—you've got to take me by Tekla's house."

"Look, Val, it's almost eleven. You have school tomorrow. We all have school. Does Tekla know you're coming? Is she expecting you?"

"No," Val answered, "but if the lights aren't on, I won't ring the bell."

"You? At this hour? Have you run away again?" Tekla Reis asked when she opened her door and found Valerie standing there.

Val shook her head. She examined Tekla, who was wrapped in a plaid wool robe that was so long its hem dragged on the floor. "No, I'm just stopping by. Bennett is with me, and his girlfriend."

"I don't see them."

"They're at the end of the alley in the car. They probably want to sit there and make out."

"Well—come on in," Tekla told her.

"I won't stay long," Val said, reaching up and tugging at a strand of her hair. She could smell the smoke from the bonfire. "Were you asleep?"

"Do you care? No, you don't care. Besides, I never sleep."

"Don't you?"

"Valerie, let's dispense with the small talk. Please. I think you should tell me why you're here and what you want."

Val followed Tekla and the oversized plaid robe into the redwood living room. The only light was a floor lamp next to the couch, which held scattered heaps of papers and a mohair afghan. In the fireplace a single log flamed with a cool, unenthusiastic glow. It was an artificial log. Duraflame. Val wanted to laugh or to cry. A Duraflame log certainly didn't make a very poetic blaze.

Tekla, not looking concerned about being poetic, settled back into her nest on the couch and began to examine Valerie. Valerie lowered her eyes and placed herself on the edge of the brick hearth facing in Tekla's direction. All of a sudden she was cold. She hunched her shoulders, and some of the now-icy rhinestone stars touched the back of her neck. She shuddered. Pulling Wendy's sweatshirt from around her shoulders, she wriggled into it. She was still cold. Her teeth were chattering now, and she didn't know how to begin.

"Would you like some hot milk?" Tekla asked.

Val looked up. She blinked. Hot milk? What a disgusting yet motherly thing to offer. Tekla had a stainless-steel thermos on the table next to her and two yellow mugs.

"If you need a clean cup, get one from the kitchen. Otherwise, you can drink out of Lenny's—the one she used before she went off to bed."

"I'll drink out of Lenny's," Valerie replied, aware that it was probably Lenore who'd prepared the thermos.

Tekla poured the milk. She leaned forward and held it out for Valerie. "I feel I owe you an apology. I was less than cordial the last time you were here. And too harsh, I think, about your writing. But reading it made me feel panicky, worried that no one else would be honest with you."

Val stood and reached for the mug. Its heat stung her chilled fingertips. She sat down again, readjusted her grip, and cleared her throat. "It's okay. You did the right thing, and I came tonight because I wanted to tell you that I've burned it."

"You do have a penchant for melodrama," Tekla commented. "And a disdain for moderation. Still, I'm sorry you destroyed it. And you'll be sorry, too."

"It was terrible."

"I was too harsh. Even if it wasn't publishable, you should have kept it. As some kind of record, or as a *memento mori*, if for no other reason."

Valerie took a sip of the scalded milk. Disgusting. She took a second sip, and it wasn't much better. She picked a clot of milk scum off her tongue and wiped her fingers on her pants. "I also came because I wanted to ask you about the baby. The one you were pregnant with before I was born."

Tekla's face was blank, unreadable.

"Was it my father's child, yours and my father's?"

Tekla took a sip from her mug, leaving a milky mustache across her upper lip. She swiped at it with the back of her hand. "No. I'd been living in Florence for almost a year. It was someone else's. A man I saw while I was there."

"What happened to the baby?"

"There was no baby. I miscarried midway through my third month. It must have been contagious—something I caught from being around your mother. Now, what else?"

Valerie leaned her head to one side and took a deep breath. "Are you in love with my father?"

"No . . . in love is different. But I care. Deeply. We're old friends. We have a history, and sometimes you care about a person and keep on caring, even when it doesn't make sense in any rational way. But it's different from being *in love*."

"Is it?"

"Yes."

Slowly, searching for the right words, Valerie began to speak. "If you feel very strongly—as you just said you do—then I think you should stay away from my dad. You're making him and my mother unhappy."

Tekla nodded. "I know." She sighed and picked at a loose thread in her robe.

"Tekla?"

"Hmm?"

"Will you stay away from my father?"

"I thought you called me T.J. like the rest of my friends."

Valerie put the mug down on the hearth. She stood up and began to move away. "I don't know whether we're friends or not," she said.

Tekla stood up, too. "I deserve that. Okay. Done. I'll stay away from your dad. From him and your mom, too. T.J.'s curse. I seem to spread a gloomy cloud wherever I go. Still, I didn't start this. It was your dad—when he called to say he thought you had literary talent that should be nurtured. And, despite what I said about your ill-conceived novel, I think he's right. Forget Molly Moore and magic butter churns. Begin at the beginning. Write from your gut."

"Maybe I'm really not any good."

Tekla raised one eyebrow. "Maybe you aren't. If you're not willing to try, though, to risk failure, how will you ever find out?"

Then, frowning, she followed Valerie toward the door. When she reached it, she turned the iron knob and threw it open. A gust of cold, damp night air blew across the threshold.

" 'Take heart, take heart, O Bulkington! Bear thee grimly . . .' "

"What?" Val asked. "My father quoted that, too. What *is* it?"

"*Moby-Dick*. Chapter twenty-three. Long ago, I wrote a poem called 'Three Twenty-thirds.' It used that and a passage from the twenty-third chapter of *Jane Eyre*, about a string that Rochester imagined tied between his heart and Jane's, and then that lush line from the Twenty-third Psalm—'My cup runneth over.' But that was something I wrote in another life and when I was another person."

As Valerie stood in the doorway, she examined the fine hair on Tekla's cheeks and upper lip. "Can I ask you something else? Just one more question?"

"Sure."

"Is my father in love with you?"

Tekla leaned her head to one side. She bit down on her bottom lip. "If you want to know that, you'll have to ask him."

Valerie turned away.

"Val, don't be angry. Please. You're a very interesting young woman, and it would be nice if, every once in a while, we could still see each other."

Val shook her head. "It hurts my mother too much when I spend time with you. Maybe even more than when my dad does."

"Don't just walk off. I'd like to keep up with your writing. And you. Wait. That's it. I know—you think all I care about is your father. You're wrong, of course."

"Am I?"

"Yes. But you're right about your mom, so this may not be the time. But maybe someday . . ."

"Maybe someday," Val echoed, lowering her eyes and beginning to walk toward Bennett's car.

"Val?"

Valerie paused. "What?"

Tekla Reis's long shadow was rippling out the door and stretching across the pavement. When Val looked down, she saw that the crown of the shadow stopped just short of her feet. Aware of a dull pain in the hollow of her chest, unsure of whether she wanted to take a step forward or a step back, she shifted her weight from one hip to the other.

"Tell the truth and tell it from the gut," Tekla called softly. "And, Val, one more thing?"

Valerie stepped back. The pain increased. "What?"

"You should wear more pink. It makes you look alive. And you are alive . . . delightfully, exuberantly alive."

# 15

*Shrugging, Tekla replied, "No, not in love. But I care a lot. You see, we're old friends, and sometimes you keep on caring about a person, even if it doesn't make sense. But that's different from being in love."*

*Suddenly, Valerie realized she had . . .*

". . . asked the wrong question. How could I have been so stupid? I blew it. She wouldn't have lied to me."

Valerie had been writing, and now she was thinking aloud, preparing herself for the talk she wanted to have with her father. He was home from the hospital. He'd been home for two days already, long enough to settle in and begin to get impatient. He wasn't complaining about the colostomy bag, but he was irritable because his incision hurt and he was feeling so tired.

Although it was Sunday, Claire had gone to the bank to catch up on paperwork that had accumulated during the week of Stan's surgery. Valerie's instructions had been to make her father lunch, to see that he got rest, and to avoid agitating him. With a sigh, she pulled herself to her feet.

Then, leaving her desk, she padded barefoot down the hallway, aware of the sound of the TV coming from the living room. Slowly she edged closer to the doorway. A man, using an exaggerated stage whisper, was talking about something called the leader board and the traps on the seventeenth. Golf. Her father was so restless, he'd watch the televised version of a game he'd never played or cared about at all. Or did he? What was her father really like? Was he a happy person? Or had his life been shadowed by a love affair from which he'd never recovered? Did Val know him or anything about him? How could anyone know a parent?

As Valerie was ruminating, she realized she was hearing a second voice lacing in and out of the stage-whispered one. It was Stan's. He was sprawled on the couch with the telephone on his chest, speaking into the receiver in a low murmur. Valerie was tempted to stay and eavesdrop, but she forced herself to head for the kitchen and begin to make his lunch. Still, even as she cracked eggs into the skillet, she couldn't help wondering who he was addressing in those confidential tones. Tekla Reis. T.J. His Jane—the woman whose ribs were tied to his with an invisible string. Val couldn't think of anyone else it could be. How, she wondered, did a person do Jacob's ladder on a telephone? Could interwoven voices be as intimate as shadows on a wall?

She was annoyed with herself but puzzled, also. She'd wasted time imagining Tekla could be her mother, yet she'd been too half-witted to catch on to the complicated relationship that existed between Tekla and her father. Tekla had promised she'd stay away from him, and Val trusted her. Still, Stan hadn't made any promises. Even now he might be betraying Claire as he whispered secrets into Tekla Reis's ear. Well, Val wasn't going to tolerate it. Claire, who was so much more vulnerable than she had imagined, was her mother. Poor Claire. How would it feel to be living her life? Wasn't it terrible to love a man who was still attached to another woman? A man who might one day leave her for that woman and whose daughter was disloyal enough to prefer that woman to her?

Val needed to take action. Since her eavesdropping days were over, however, she knew she'd have to be more direct. So, as she stepped into the living room with the tray of eggs and applesauce, she was careful to rattle it to alert Stan that she was coming. Lifting his head, flushing, he said a hushed, affectionate goodbye and hung up the phone.

" 'You are my sunshine,' " Stan sang softly, drumming his fingers across the top of the phone, " 'my only sunshine . . .' "

Valerie slid the tray onto the coffee table in front of the couch and seated herself on the floor across from him. She folded her hands.

He raised one eyebrow. "Looks good. Yummy scrambled eggs and Gerber's applesauce."

"You're supposed to have bland food," she said. "Besides, that's what Mom told me to fix."

"Okay, okay. Truce. And, wait a minute—look at you. You're wearing something other than black for a change. You look pretty in pink. *Pretty in Pink*. Wasn't that the name of a movie?"

"Yes," Val answered, wishing she hadn't put on Wendy's glittery sweatshirt again. She passed a plate to her father and picked up the other one for herself.

Stan rested his plate back on his chest. "Hey, what's

going on with you? You're stiff as a board. I thought your mom said you'd had a good talk, that we'd gotten all the nonsense behind us and were going to get on with our lives."

"That's right."

"And you're going to apply yourself again at school?"

"Yes, I promised Mr. Litke I'd pay attention to all his David Copperfield 'I am born' stuff. And I also wrote Molly Moore—she won't take my calls anymore—and told her I don't have anything for her to publish right now, because I burned the novel I was writing."

"But?" Stan asked. "So what is it? What's still on your mind?"

Valerie put down her plate, too. "Tekla," she said.

Her father frowned. "What about her? If you accept the fact that she's not your mother, what can you possibly want to know?"

Leaning forward, Val stared into her father's eyes. This time she wasn't going to ask about being "in love." This time she was going to get the question right. "Do you love Tekla Reis?"

For a moment, Stan lay there in silence, stroking his chin. When he finally spoke, his voice was very quiet. "Valerie, listen to me. Listen to what I am about to tell you—and remember it. I love your mother. She's warm and comforting and—instead of spreading gloom—she brings sunshine wherever she goes. She's calm, cheerful. A steady dose of good weather. It's a pleasure. Remember what T.J. said at the Elite about how a mountain climber describes a particularly dangerous piece of rock as 'very interesting'? Well, it's a favorite image of hers. She likes the world that way. But I can't live on a rocky ledge in the midst of thunderstorms and hurricane-force winds. I can't keep battling that on a daily basis."

Valerie thought about hurricanes and other kinds of violent weather. She thought about poetry and passion, play-readings and shadows on the wall. Then she considered the quiet afterglow of a sunset. It was hard to believe that good weather, while soothing, was as moving or exciting as a volcano erupting or a thunderstorm in the mountains.

"I know you love Mom," Val continued, still thinking. "But, Daddy, do you love Tekla, too? Did you sleep with her? Do you sleep with her as well as with Mom? *Do you love her?*"

Stan reached out and took hold of the plate of now cold eggs. He began to eat, chewing in a perfunctory manner, then swallowing. "I'm sorry," he said at last. "I'm not going to answer those questions. Not because I have anything to hide, but because I'm your father, and you have to trust me."

"But, Daddy—"

"Quiet, please, and let me finish. Even when I make a mistake—like the mistake of asking Tekla to take a look at your writing—it's an inadvertent one. But I am a worrier. Therefore colitis and surgery and, now, an effort to worry less. And you, I think, are a worrier, too. Still, Val, you're just going to have to trust that I love you, that I love your mother, and wouldn't intentionally do anything to hurt either of you."

Val leaned her head to one side. She frowned.

"If you don't believe me, Ducky, you don't. That's too bad. There are, however, such things in this world—as pretentious as it may sound—as honor and discretion. I'd like to think I'm an honorable person, a person of discretion. And I'd also like to say that there are still a few things that are totally inappropriate to discuss with one's teenaged daughter. And this is one of them." Stan paused. He gazed at Val. "Now . . . do you have any other questions?"

Yes, of course she had other questions. Dozens of them, but she wasn't going to ask them. Not now. Maybe never.

"No," she said, rocking forward onto her knees. She pulled herself to her feet. For a moment, undecided, she stood looking down at Stan. She backed up. She might not understand her father, but she felt very close to him. Impulsively, she swooped forward, grabbed hold of his hands, and began kissing him on the top of his head. When she noticed his eyebrows wriggling with embarrassment over the lavishness of her gestures, she dropped his hands and reminded him that he was supposed to rest.

"Maybe I'll swim," she said, as she lifted the tray, "while you sleep. By the time you wake up, Mom and I will both be home."

She believed Stan, she told herself, as she was in the kitchen sliding the dishes into the dishwasher. She did, but she felt tense again and unsettled. She was sure her father *was* an honorable person, but who had he been talking to on the telephone? Why were things that should be so simple so complicated?

Valerie swam lap after lap, not counting, just swimming. Freestyle. Breaststroke. Backstroke. The water was unusually warm, and clouds of steam swirled through the air above her head. When she lay on her back, she noticed that the overhead lights reminded her of the operating room when she'd had her tonsils out. Stan had been there when she'd gone under the anesthetic. Claire, too. Claire smiling calmly down at her, her round face shining and soothing. "Inhale. Blow the gas up on the lights," she'd told her. "Coat them with it."

Remembering, Val rolled over into a front crawl. Tendrils of her hair unspiraled in the warm, comforting, supportive water. She also saw the odd, jewel-like facets of the surface crazing the bottom of the pool and the shadows of her hands as they tried to make contact with the warm, bluish pink ones dangling at the ends of her wrists.

As Val swam, she kept thinking about her parents and about Tekla Reis. Considering the three of them—separately and together—she watched the lights and her bluish, slightly enlarged hands, the same hands that held the pen and paper when she wrote. Write from the gut, Tekla had said. The awareness that she and Tekla wouldn't be seeing each other made Val's chest tighten. She'd made the right decision, but—still—she'd lost something of value. And she'd never had a chance to ask what writing from the gut meant. Now she couldn't. She suspected it had something to do with earthquakes and tornadoes. But the earthquakes and tornadoes that she'd actually experienced, not the ones she'd read about in the newspaper or seen clips of on television.

Concentrating, Valerie churned through the water, stretching herself toward a euphoric state of adrenaline-charged exhaustion. She was almost there, twisting expectantly into a somersault turn, when someone called her name. The person hailing her was sitting at the deep end of the pool, dangling a pair of white feet in the water.

Val completed the turn. Then, stretching out her arms, she doubled back, wriggling toward the sixty-foot marker. A woman was waiting for her. Stan's sunshine. His only sunshine. The only person in the world he could have been addressing on the phone in those touching, private tones.

"How did you know I was here?"

"Your father called back and told me. He said you were upset. And I thought you'd feel better if you saw me."

"I do," Valerie replied, aware of a relaxed warmth spreading through her body that had little to do with adrenaline-induced euphoria. "Sometimes things seem so difficult and confusing."

"They can be. But sometimes we make them more difficult than they need to be."

Val nodded. "Especially me."

"No, all of us, I'm afraid."

Tugging off her goggles, Val flicked water away from her eyes. "Mommy, oh, Mommy . . ."

Claire leaned her round, pale face down toward Val. Her stomach protruded as if she'd wedged a small foam rubber pillow inside the front of her boy-legged swimsuit. Her calves were freckled. Her toenails were neatly clipped. Remembering something, Valerie stared at the toes.

"What's wrong?"

"Your toes. I have toes just like yours," Valerie said, aware that she felt too shaky at that moment to do something as simple as apologize for the pain she'd caused. She pulled herself from the pool and watched as water dribbled off her and spread under Claire's dry suit. "I've searched and searched for some way we look alike, and here it is. My baby toes curve up and lap over just like yours."

"That's what the doctor said when you were born: 'Well, who's got the weird toes?' "

"Why didn't you tell me?"

Claire cleared her throat, but her cheek didn't twitch. Then she smiled at Valerie. "Because, Ducky, there are some things that you simply have to discover for yourself." She wrapped one arm around Val's shoulders and sniffed. "Oh, it smells wonderful in here and brings back all kinds of memories. Just like your laundry when you were a baby—so clean and so new . . ."

Valerie nodded. Reminded unexpectedly of the color of a winter sunrise, she edged closer to her mother. How hard it must be sometimes to be Claire, smoothing out real feelings and glossing over them with cheerfulness. Still, it was a strength, too. Thinking, Val closed her eyes and thought of the ocean on a windless day, reflecting the edge of a round, pale sun.

She opened her eyes. "I didn't mean to hurt you."

"I know."

"But I was crazed—about being an author, about myself. I wasn't myself. But I am now, and I'm really sorry."

Claire's face was pensive, warm yet self-contained.

"I may be an author," Val continued, "although not a famous one—just an ordinary one who goes to school and has a family—but I've got to find out if I can become a writer. Do you think that's possible?"

"Definitely," Claire said. "I have faith in you. Even

to me—or especially to me—you are a young woman of infinite possibilities."

Grateful, Val kneaded the soft flesh of her mother's thigh. "I'm going to cut my hair, too. Short—really short. Like Wendy's."

"Who's Wendy?"

"Bennett's new girlfriend. The one who gave me the pink sweatshirt."

"Her name is Winnie," Claire said.

"Winnie—her name is Winnie? *Winnie?* I need to listen better. Only I can make that kind of mistake. But I'm going to change. I'm going to pay more attention. I must."

"Why?" Claire asked, leaning over to nuzzle Val's cheek.

"Because—stop, that tickles—I'll need to start paying attention to everything. And as soon as possible. For instance, did you—as Bennett says—really sew sequins on your figure-skating costumes? And what made you give up skating?"

"I got too fat."

"Oh, Mom . . ."

Claire stared at her toes and at Val's. She smiled. "It's okay. I didn't mind. I hated sequins anyway. Always did. Only DeDe liked them."

Suddenly Val remembered a fading color picture of her mother in a twinkling blue outfit with one leg extended above her head. Then she thought of herself and of the sound of the starting gun echoing above the surface of the swimming pool. "Didn't you miss the wonderful, horrible feeling of competing?"

"I'm not sure. It's so long ago, and I seldom think about it. But I will, if you want me to. And I'll tell you what I remember. The bad things as well as the good. Is that what you want?"

"Yes," Valerie said. "Yes."

Because she needed to listen, to learn. Notice detail. Absorb. Probe for something that wasn't a trick and wasn't done with mirrors. She was, she felt, poised on a particularly dangerous yet interesting piece of rock. She'd have to be ruthlessly honest, too. Tell the truth. How else would she ever begin to find out what it meant to write from the gut?

# 16

*I was born. It was midnight on a Tuesday, and my parents' lives were already intertwined with the life of a moody, difficult poet named Tekla Reis . . .*